A QUIET PLACE

Seichō Matsumoto

Translated by Louise Heal Kawai

BITTER LEMON PRESS
LONDON

BITTER LEMON PRESS
First published in the United Kingdom in 2016 by
Bitter Lemon Press, 47 Wilmington Square, London WC1X 2ET

www.bitterlemonpress.com

First published in Japanese as *Kikanakatta Basho* by
Kadokawa Corporation, Tokyo, 1975

English translation rights arranged with Kadokawa Corporation,
Tokyo through The English Agency (Japan) Ltd.

Bitter Lemon Press gratefully acknowledges the financial
assistance of the Arts Council of England

A CIP record for this book is available from the British Library

ISBN 978-1-908524-63-8
eBook ISBN: 978-1-908524-64-5

Typeset by Tetragon, London
Printed and bound by CPI Group (UK) Ltd, Croydon, CRO 4YY

Supported using public funding by
ARTS COUNCIL
ENGLAND
LOTTERY FUNDED

1

Tsuneo Asai was on a business trip to the Kansai region when he heard the news.

Around 8.30 in the evening, he was having dinner and drinks in the banquet room of a high-class restaurant with businessmen from the food processing industry. Asai was a section chief in the Staple Food Department of the Ministry of Agriculture and Forestry. He'd arrived in Kobe the day before, accompanying the ministry's brand-new director general on a tour of inspection. It had only been a month since Director-General Shiraishi had been promoted from a different department, and he wasn't very familiar with the practicalities of the job as yet. For the past couple of days, he and Asai had been visiting canning facilities and ham-processing plants in the Osaka–Kobe area, and were off to Hiroshima the next day. This evening they were enjoying the hospitality of some of the local business owners.

The evening was starting to wind down. Shiraishi, who was three years Asai's senior, was sitting across from the chairman of the Food Manufacturers' Association. The two men were discussing golf. The director general was known for his low handicap. In addition, he was an expert at *shogi* – Japanese chess – and Go, and a legend within the ministry for his mah-jong skills. Asai was at his side, sipping sake, pretending to be absorbed in his boss's story. He believed that listening faithfully to one's manager's idle chit-chat was a mark of respect. Shiraishi's voice was getting louder, oiled by the whisky he was drinking. He'd made director general by the age of forty-five – a rapid rise through the ranks. Unlike Asai, Shiraishi had graduated from the law department of the elite Tokyo University, and was a favourite of the vice-minister, leader of one of the ministry's main political factions.

In advance of the personnel change, Asai had approached the manufacturers to warn them that the incoming director general was only planning a two-year – well, maybe as little as a year and a half – temporary stop-over in the post before transferring back into one of the ministry's mainstream departments, and wouldn't be putting much effort into the job.

"He won't be at all familiar with the business side of things," Asai explained. "But don't worry; he'll rely on me for everything. Leave him to me. Now, it's possible he might try to pull off some sort of impressive stunt to draw more attention to himself, but I'll be right there as a guide. I'll be able to rein him in, don't you worry."

The manufacturers, anxious to gain their government certification, were all too happy to defer to Asai's veteran experience. Asai had developed a pretty cosy relationship with them, but he never let it show while Director-General Shiraishi was around. Shiraishi had spent his free time at Tokyo University brushing up on his Go, *shogi*, mah-jong and golf; Asai, the kid from a poor family who'd struggled to graduate from a small private university and work his way up through the civil service ranks, was an entirely different species.

There were also about twenty geishas in attendance; the life and soul of the party knelt on a cushion across from the director general. It turned out that she was a golfer too, and she'd joined in their conversation about scores. The party was starting to wind down, and her placement directly opposite Shiraishi looked suspiciously like the work of the vice-chairman of the local Association of Food Manufacturers, Mr Yagishita. At least that was what Asai reckoned. Yagishita was a big name in the ham- and sausage-manufacturing business. A little while earlier, Asai had seen him carefully observing the director general's reaction to the geisha. He must have now got up from his spot by the chairman and come around to whisper in Asai's ear.

But it wasn't Yagishita who was whispering in his ear. It was one of the waitresses.

"There's a telephone call for you from Tokyo."

Asai didn't get up right away. It would be disrespectful to the director general for him to rush off. He picked up his cup of sake from the table and took a sip. Still feigning interest in his boss's golfing tale, he wondered what could be so important for someone to call him this late. He'd been on all kinds of business trips, but his wife, Eiko, practically never called him. And she was his only family member. Whenever Asai went off on a long trip, she would invite her younger sister to stay and keep her company. This was a five-day trip, so Asai's sister-in-law ought to be there. He could think of no reason for Eiko to need to get in touch with him. He'd been out during the day, of course, but what could possibly be so urgent for her to call the restaurant?

After about a minute, Asai rose slowly from his floor cushion. His boss was facing away from him, in conversation with the chairman. The geisha glanced his way, but quickly turned her attention back to the director general. Around twenty-seven or -eight, round-cheeked, she was definitely Shiraishi's type.

Outside the party room, Asai followed the waitress along the corridor, around two corners to a glass-doored telephone booth. The receiver was off the hook.

"Hello, it's me," he began, but there was no one on the other end. His heart began to beat harder. He could hear other voices in the background, too faint to make out the words, but there was definitely some sort of commotion. Close by, he thought he could hear a woman sobbing. He recognized it as the voice of his sister-in-law, Miyako. That was why there had been no response – Miyako was in tears.

"Miyako! What's the matter?" There was a slight tremor in his voice. He realized that something must have happened to Eiko for her not to come to the phone in person.

"Eiko's…"

Asai couldn't really follow the rest. Miyako was so emotional it was hard to tell whether she was laughing or crying.

Then he thought he made out the word "dead".

"What?" he asked. "What did you say?"

"Eiko's dead."

"Dead? Are you sure?"

A waitress passed by in the corridor outside the glass booth. The door was tightly closed, and she didn't even glance at him.

"When?"

Miyako's speech was distorted by a huge wave of sobbing.

"Just over four hours ago."

She'd been dead for more than four hours, and he was only just hearing about it? When he left for his trip he'd made sure to write down his schedule and the telephone numbers of the hotels he'd be staying at. Miyako would have called the hotel and been given the number of the restaurant. She should have called him here right away. There must have been an accident – that would have caused a delay. And it couldn't have happened at home – she must have died elsewhere, otherwise Miyako would have called him immediately. But if they'd taken her to hospital, surely someone would have called to let him know.

"Was it a traffic accident?" he asked.

"It's me." Eiko's father was on the line. "No, not a traffic accident."

So his father-in-law had already arrived from the suburbs.

"She had a heart attack. It was very sudden."

Asai's seventy-year-old father-in-law sounded shaken. He couldn't stop coughing.

"She was walking in the street, was suddenly overcome with pain, and collapsed in a nearby shop. The owner called Miyako and she got a taxi straight there, but it was already too late."

"Did the shopkeeper call an ambulance?"

Asai was struggling to keep his emotions under control.

"No, she didn't. There was a private clinic about two hundred yards away, so she got the doctor to come right over, but Eiko's heart had already stopped beating."

Eiko had a weak heart. She'd already suffered a mild heart attack two years ago.

"Where is she now?"

"They brought her back to the house about an hour ago. Miyako called your hotel to find out where you were."

He could still hear Miyako weeping, and what sounded like his brother-in-law in the background, too.

"So what train will you be coming back on?" Eiko's father asked.

"There won't be any more bullet trains this evening. I'll fly back if I can make it to the airport in time. Otherwise it'll be the overnight train that gets into Tokyo in the morning."

"We'll all be waiting. I just can't believe it. It's such a shock. You should…"

His father-in-law had been going to tell him to try to stay calm and come home, but his voice petered out. It was almost as if the pain of causing trouble for his son-in-law was harder to deal with than the death of his daughter.

Asai left the telephone booth and called over one of the waitresses.

"Can I make it to the airport to catch a Tokyo flight tonight?"

The waitress folded back the violet-coloured sleeve of her kimono and looked at her wristwatch.

"It's almost ten past nine now. The last flight is at nine thirty, so I doubt it."

The restaurant was used to hosting customers from the capital, so they knew the flight times by heart.

"Do you need to get back right away?"

"Yes. What about an express train?"

"There's one leaving from Sannomiya at quarter past ten. It gets into Tokyo around 9.30 in the morning."

"I'll get that one. Could you call me a cab?"

"For one person?"

"Yes, just me. It's an emergency."

As he headed back towards the restaurant, he decided he'd ask Vice-Chairman Yagishita of the Food Manufacturers' Association to take care of Shiraishi. There was no way he could ask the ministry to send a replacement. His boss was going to have to complete the last two days of the tour of inspection by himself. For a man who liked to appear grand and dignified it would be insufferable not to have an assistant on a job like this. Perhaps he should ask for someone from the Hiroshima branch office… But if it wasn't someone from headquarters, well, it wouldn't be respectful to either the director general or the businessmen…

Not even the shock of losing his wife could completely distract Asai from work matters.

When he returned to the banquet room, they'd reached the final, rice course. His manager was busily eating a bowl of *ochazuke* rice with sea bream and green tea. The round-cheeked geisha was still attending to him. She watched Asai bow to Shiraishi and reseat himself before offering him the choice of *ochazuke* or plain steamed rice.

Asai had been gone quite a long time, and as he looked at his boss's profile he detected a look of displeasure. He sat and fiddled with his hot rice bowl, wondering how best to approach the subject. He didn't really have time to waste; Miyako's weeping still echoed in his ears.

He carefully placed the bowl of untouched *ochazuke* on the table, pushed himself up to a kneeling position and shuffled a little closer to the director general.

"Mr Shiraishi, sir," he said in a low voice, "I am very sorry to have to tell you —"

His boss inclined his head almost imperceptibly in Asai's direction.

"I'm hoping to keep this private from the rest of the party…"

Things were not quite as lively as when the alcohol had been served earlier, but the party was still in full swing.

"Anyhow, I just received a phone call from my home in Tokyo. It seems my wife passed away unexpectedly."

Shiraishi didn't appear to have heard properly, and leaned in a little closer, a puzzled expression on his face.

"A heart attack. A few hours ago."

This time, the director general understood. His eyes widened and he hurriedly placed his rice bowl on the table. His gaze darted quickly around the room before settling on Asai's face.

"Really? Well, I'm —" His voice had taken on an appropriately sombre tone.

"It's true, I'm afraid," Asai added, in barely more than a murmur. "I just heard it from my father- and sister-in-law."

"Was she in poor health, then, your wife?" asked his boss, adjusting his own voice to Asai's level.

"No, sir, she was in good health. She had a sudden heart attack while out walking, and collapsed in a nearby shop. She died on the spot, apparently."

"Well, that's, er…"

As Asai had asked him to keep the news from the rest of the party, Shiraishi lowered his head slightly. His earlier look of irritation had quickly turned to a mixture of sympathy and unease.

"Well, you'd better get back to Tokyo straight away." He issued the order in a low voice.

"Oh, thank you, sir. I'm terribly sorry that I won't be able to be of service to you any longer on this trip."

"Oh, please. Don't worry about it. Well..." He checked his watch. "There won't be any more flights tonight."

"Right."

"Are there any trains?"

"I heard from the restaurant staff that there'll be an overnight train at 10.15."

"Well, that doesn't give you very much time. I'll be fine. You'd better get on your way."

"Thank you very much. I'm so sorry for all the inconvenience I'm causing you."

"No, don't be. It's nothing at all."

The food-processing reps were eating and drinking as normal, but they were throwing the occasional glance in the direction of the two men speaking in whispers. The geisha had taken her cue to leave, and was quietly chatting with one of her fellow entertainers.

"I'm very sorry about this."

"I'll come and pay my respects to your family once I'm back in Tokyo."

"Oh no, sir, that's not necessary... Well, I appreciate it. I know how busy you are."

"Anyway, you'd better get going. After you're gone, I'll find the right moment to explain to everybody."

"Oh no, sir. Please don't trouble yourself. I'll call Vice-Chairman Yagishita out into the hallway, and explain the situation to him. I'll get him to tell the others."

"Oh, all right then."

The director general accepted without hesitation. He looked decidedly relieved not to have to perform such an unpleasant task himself.

"About the rest of the tour, sir. For the Hiroshima inspections, shall I ask the director of the General Affairs division at the local office to accompany you? If that's acceptable to you, I can ask Yagishita to arrange it."

"Please don't worry about all that. I'll manage just fine."

"But if we don't sort it out right away —"

"Never mind. Just get on your way. You still have to go and pick up your things from the hotel, don't you?"

"Oh, yes... Well, I suppose I'd better take my leave."

Now everyone had noticed that something was going on. Thirty pairs of eyes followed Asai as he got to his feet. He shot Yagishita a look and hurried out into the corridor. Yagishita followed right behind.

The vice-chairman was astounded to hear Asai's story. To save time, the two of them talked on their way towards the exit.

"I thought it was a bit strange, all that whispering between you and the director general, but I never imagined it could be anything so awful. I don't know what to say."

Yagishita lowered his balding head and bowed deeply to Asai.

"Thanks. It was a complete shock."

"It must have been. Like a bad dream, I suppose. When I tell everyone I reckon they'll all be pretty shocked too."

"I didn't think it appropriate for me to announce it during dinner, but could you find the right moment and let everyone know?"

"Of course I will, don't you worry. But Mr Asai, there was no need to hold back. We've all known you for years! You should feel at home here."

"I'm sorry – I do have one more request. After I leave, the director general will be travelling by himself. I don't suppose you could suggest someone to look after him? It's too late to get anyone from the ministry, but tomorrow morning could you give the Hiroshima office a call and get the director of General Affairs to meet him at the station and stay with him for the rest of the trip?"

"Got it. But you really shouldn't be worrying about work at a time like this."

There was pity in Yagishita's voice.

"No, no. It's fine. It's my job, after all. I have to hand over the reins in a responsible manner. I can't be seen to get distracted by personal matters."

"But your wife has passed away. It's completely different."

"I suppose so. But I still have to make a distinction between personal and professional matters. After I leave, the director general is going to be all alone, and that's not going to make him look good at all."

"Yeah, well, I suppose you're right, but —"

"Anyway, could you do that for me?"

"Sure. No problem. Have a safe trip home!"

Asai stopped walking for a moment and leaned to whisper in Yagishita's ear.

"What do you think about the girl sitting across from Mr Shiraishi? Do you think anything's going to come of that?"

Yagishita looked stunned. Apparently, when it came to his bosses, nothing escaped Asai's attention.

"Mr Asai. You're not worrying yourself about that sort of thing at a time like this, are you?"

It wasn't until much later that Asai finally began to recover from the shock. Rattled around by the movement of the overnight train, he lay awake and began to think. Where had Eiko been when she'd had the heart attack? He'd forgotten to ask.

2

Following Eiko's funeral, Asai observed the seventh-day Buddhist memorial service, but once that was over the house felt empty. It'd be a long time before everyone would get together again. There'd be the next memorial on the first anniversary of her death, but Asai wasn't sure how many of Eiko's relatives were likely to turn up. He and Eiko had no children, so it felt as if the family line had ended with her death.

Asai and Eiko's marriage had lasted seven years. They'd married a year after Asai's first wife had passed away. He'd been thirty-five, and she eight years his junior. At twenty-seven, it was Eiko's first marriage. The matchmaker told him that she'd been very picky early on about who she'd accept a marriage proposal from, and that gradually her chances of finding someone had faded. When they first came face to face, Asai had guessed that was true. She wasn't all that great-looking, but he was attracted by her cheerful smile.

Asai had expressed a strong interest in Eiko, perhaps because his first wife had been rather plain-looking. However, the matchmaker didn't bring him an immediate acceptance of his proposal. Eiko had hesitated. He hadn't been sure if it was something to do with her age – twenty-seven was late for a first marriage – or if it had been a problem for her that it was his second. Asai also knew he wasn't exactly a great looker himself; he'd never been popular with the ladies. The only thing really going for him was the stability of his job as a civil servant, but even that didn't pay a great salary.

Finally, after keeping him in suspense for a good while, Eiko had agreed to marry him. Asai loved her. His second wife was much younger and more immature than his first, and he treated her more like a favourite child. Sometimes the age difference felt a lot closer to a dozen years.

Eiko, for her part, rather enjoyed being spoiled by her affectionate husband. It wasn't uncommon for her to spend two or three days at a time lying on the sofa, claiming to be too tired to do any housework. Asai never complained. He'd go out shopping and do all the cooking and cleaning himself.

Whenever she was feeling fatigued, Eiko wouldn't let Asai anywhere near her. She'd never been particularly into sex. This didn't mean she wasn't affectionate to her husband – she just wasn't very assertive in bed. It was a little disappointing to Asai, but it didn't stop him from adoring his young wife.

Eiko was very sociable and loved to spend time with friends. This aspect of her personality contrasted strongly with how quiet she was at home. She had two completely different sides. Asai often wondered if she was bored staying at home with him. She certainly came to life whenever she went out somewhere.

Mostly she spent time with women she'd known for years, and friends of those friends. At the beginning they'd all studied traditional Japanese ballads together. Somewhere along the line they'd quit those classes, and switched to playing the shamisen. Next it had been Japanese-style painting. Most recently, Eiko had been studying haiku with a woman poet in Suginami Ward. One of her friends who had been a pupil there for some time had invited her to join the class. She didn't seem to be able to stick with things for long, but Asai supposed, as a result, her life was never monotonous.

Happily, the haiku infatuation seemed to have stuck. Eiko had already been studying it for two years, with no sign of giving up. She even seemed to have a small amount of talent for it, and her poems were often praised by her teacher and fellow pupils. From time to time, she'd have a poem chosen for publication in an amateur haiku fan magazine. Eiko's teachers had praised her shamisen playing and her painting in the past, but actually seeing her own work in print had encouraged her more than anything. Being average at something was depressing; to be top of her class put her in great spirits. She always enjoyed comparing her results to other people's. She had cleared her desk at home of all her paints and brushes, and for a while now it had been covered in books – collections of haiku poetry, glossaries of terms, dictionaries.

Apparently, the women who wrote haiku were either very old or very young; there weren't many in between. Women around Eiko's age – in their mid-thirties – were usually housewives with two or three children and found it difficult to get away, so Eiko and three or four of her friends were the only ones of that generation who attended the meetings.

It was about two or three years ago that Eiko had turned to her husband and asked, out of the blue, "Do you think I'm sexy?"

Asai had asked if someone had told her she was, to which she'd replied that a fellow haiku poet had told her that she was very sexy – not in any vulgar way, but that she had a kind of glamour about her. She'd clearly been delighted.

"Was it a man or a woman who told you that?" Asai was very conscious of the fact that there were far more men than women in her haiku circle.

"Of course it was a woman! I never talk to the men about anything but poetry. There's no one who'd say anything like that to me. But this woman said that if she could see it, then it must be obvious to men too."

Because Asai was around her day in day out, he hadn't really noticed, but when Eiko had told him this he'd seen what she meant. The lines of her figure had softened and rounded. She'd always been charming, but as she approached her mid-thirties that sweetness had changed to a more mature sexiness.

"Ugh. I had a bad experience today. One of the women in my haiku circle told me she'd always assumed I was a bar hostess or something. She'd heard from one of my friends that I wasn't, but found it hard to believe. Is that how people see me? I'm going to have to start wearing frumpier clothes from now on."

But all the frumpy outfits in the world wouldn't have disguised her sex appeal; they'd have simply served to highlight the sexiness beneath the surface. To be honest, it had nothing to do with the clothes – it was her body.

What had always been her sociable and open behaviour now came across as a little flirty. Asai saw it after this conversation, even in the smallest gesture.

They say a woman in her thirties is in the prime of her life, thought Asai. It was only natural that her body would change. This exact topic had come up when Asai had been out drinking with his colleagues after work. One of his colleagues had claimed that there was nothing natural about a thirty-something woman who started to look sexier; he believed her increased sensuality was achieved through experience. The rest had agreed. There was only one way that a woman's sexuality could mature, and that was by having more sex.

But Asai had been reluctant to agree. Sex with his own wife couldn't possibly be responsible for her increased voluptuousness. Not only was it very infrequent, but there was nothing wild or adventurous about it either. He knew from frank conversations over drinks that his own sex life was only about a tenth of the frequency of his colleagues'. Assuming this group was an average cross section of the general public, he'd realized he was way, way below the norm. Eiko just wasn't interested.

To make matters worse, about two years previously, Eiko had suffered a heart attack. The unexpected pain in her chest had abruptly drained all the colour from her face, and she'd broken out in a cold sweat. She'd made it to the hospital in time, and the doctor had diagnosed a mild coronary. After a week in hospital, she'd made a full recovery, but ever since then she'd been even less keen on Asai's attentions in bed. She'd read in some medical journal that a second heart attack was likely to be fatal, so she'd resolved to take extra care. She'd said it was important to keep as calm as possible and avoid any kind of shock. That was another reason she'd taken up haiku.

The doctor had told Asai that although it was important to be cautious, that what Eiko had read in the medical journal was "textbook" advice as it were, she didn't really need to follow it to the letter. She'd had a heart attack, but it was a mild one, and being too neurotic about a recurrence was inadvisable.

Asai agreed that being neurotic was a bad thing. And probably that was the appeal of the world of haiku poetry; it was very good for her spiritual health. However, after the heart attack, she'd completely refused all physical contact, which, to be honest, she'd never been particularly enthusiastic about in the first place.

And that was why Asai had disagreed with the opinion that experience was what caused a woman's sexuality to blossom. Sex had nothing to do with it. He believed that a woman's body went through natural changes as she aged. But he couldn't express these views to other people. If he did, he'd have to cough up the truth about the woeful state of his own sex life. He realized there was no other way to make his case, but he wasn't prepared to be that open. In the end, whenever the conversation turned to this topic, he kept a poker face.

It was curious, though – and he supposed that every case was different – that because his wife's sex drive was so low, his own body and needs seemed to have adjusted to hers. He didn't seem to have any strong sexual desires any more. He could easily have paid a woman to have his own needs met, or even started an affair, but he'd never been particularly interested. He supposed it was because he and Eiko were perfectly in tune.

But besides being in tune with Eiko, there were two other reasons he wasn't interested. The first was that he was the kind of person who valued money above everything. He understood that it was vital to a stable lifestyle. He believed that being without savings was the equivalent of standing on the precipice of hell. This way of thinking came from being poor and having to work himself through college. There was no way he was going to waste a single yen of his hard-earned money on a few moments of pleasure with a prostitute. Anyway, it wasn't as easy as it had been in the past to visit a red-light district and pick up a woman. These days you had to know the right people. If you didn't, then you had to go to a bar at least three or four times and do your best to persuade some woman you met there to sleep with you or have her introduce someone to you. Not only was this a colossal waste of time and energy, it ended up being expensive. And it might have been okay when he was young, but it was hardly the behaviour of a respectable forty-something. What if he ran into some young guy from the ministry? Imagine the embarrassment! He'd be a laughing stock. And it might end up damaging his prospects at work.

Asai was immensely proud of being section chief at the Ministry of Agriculture. That was the other reason he didn't want a colourful private life. There were plenty of people who had played around, valuing their private life above work, and they'd run into trouble with the powers that be. That had been the end of promotion for them. Some had even quit the ministry altogether, and after that they'd never been able to find a decent job.

It wasn't that the ministry was the pleasantest work environment, but he mostly kept his complaints to himself. There were times when he felt extremely irritated at the elite-track types, known as "career civil servants", but this was Japanese bureaucracy, and there was nothing rational about it. If you were going to be that enraged at the system, you might as well quit. To rebel was futile.

Rather than wasting his time banging his head against the bureaucratic wall, Asai carefully planned his own route to success. With the right care and attention he'd make division chief. There were a few people with the same academic background as himself who'd become director. And once in a blue moon someone like him actually made it to director general.

To be fair, he wasn't aiming quite that high, but he at least meant to be division chief before he retired. And so he did his job diligently. He'd set out to become an expert in practical matters, to be something the elite-track director generals and division chiefs couldn't. This was his only means of competing with the highly educated, career-track types.

When he said "compete", it wasn't exactly a contest. He simply made sure he was their go-to person when it came to practical matters. The elite tended to see their position at the ministry as a kind of temporary stopover on the highway to greatness. They had no idea about the day-to-day practicalities of the job. In fact, as they were only resting briefly on their journey, they didn't even bother to familiarize themselves properly with the requirements of the job. They'd skate by, believing they'd grasped the fundamental principles, barely slowing down as they blindly rubber-stamped everything that came their way.

Asai was the loyal assistant, the faithful aide to these higher-ups, though admittedly he wasn't equally helpful to everyone. He was very adept at sniffing out whether someone was likely to rise high in the ranks or not. He'd learned this both from experience and from studying the facts.

Whenever Asai did a job for someone who didn't seem to have a very bright future, he appeared attentive enough, but his heart wasn't truly in it. There was no going above and beyond his duties. He'd surreptitiously watch and wait for the boss in question to run into difficulties, while cleverly making sure no one noticed that he was being deliberately malicious. This way, he got some of the resentment and frustration out of his system.

However, everything changed if he spotted a superior on the career fast-track. It didn't matter how mediocre a boss he might be, Asai would treat him with utter devotion, on occasion performing amazing feats on his behalf and allowing his boss to take the credit.

Division chiefs would become directors, and directors would become director generals. In the future, one of these bosses might well return to the department to be his direct supervisor once again, and then, Asai reckoned, he would be justly rewarded. Along with the increase in salary from each promotion would be a larger severance cheque and a much higher pension.

Asai poured all of his energy into his job at the ministry, so the dismal state of his marital relations with Eiko barely bothered him. Things had always been like that, and now she had her heart condition. He was used to taking care of her.

And then, with his wife's sudden death, Asai seemed to have lost his way.

He had bawled as his wife's body was laid in its coffin, and when the time came for it to pass through the little window into the crematorium furnace, his father-in-law had had to pry him off. Do all husbands who lose their beloved wives feel this way? Asai had wondered as he wiped the tears from his eyes. Does everyone feel like this? He'd surprised himself. He wasn't normally the type to show his feelings.

Surely not all of those tears were caused by a fleeting rush of emotion – he must have loved Eiko deeply. Their seven years together may not have been the richest of married lives, but having her die on him reminded him how much he'd cared about her. He was older and had seen a lot more of life, had often treated her like a child, but he was now reminded with a jolt that they'd been equal partners in marriage.

He was still working through these emotions when one Sunday, around ten days after Eiko's death, her sister came by. Miyako's husband, a technician at an oil company, was away on a two-month overseas business trip, looking into future sites for development. Miyako usually stayed with her parents while he was away, and when Asai was absent on business she'd always stayed with Eiko at her place.

"You must be feeling lonely," she said to Asai, as she lit an incense stick for her sister and offered a prayer in front of the family altar. She hesitated a little as she took a seat by Asai.

"I've still not completely come to terms with the fact that she's dead," Asai replied truthfully. "I wasn't there when she died. And it didn't even happen at home."

Asai had been at the dinner party in Kobe when Miyako had rung to let him know that Eiko was dead. He'd never been able to separate in his head the content of that phone call with where he'd been when he took the call. He'd been there in Kobe as assistant to Director-General Shiraishi, and that was where his mind had been when he'd heard the news. To be more precise, he hadn't been quite sure at that point whether Shiraishi was a dead cert for future glory. His wife was from a famous political dynasty, but her family had no strong connections in the ministry's personnel office. However, there were rumours that Mrs Shiraishi was well connected with a certain influential politician. No one knew for sure whether her husband was destined to become the top bureaucrat or whether he would be transferred out of the ministry mid-career to be an industry adviser elsewhere. Asai knew he had to be extra attentive just in case, so he'd been very tense that night. Shiraishi had been born to a privileged family and raised as the favoured son, meaning he could be too distracted and laid-back. Asai had also heard that he could be very unpredictable in his moods, so he'd been particularly alert the whole evening.

The dinner party had been lively, and each attendee had lined up to receive a cup of sake from the director general. The round-cheeked geisha had been seated opposite him. Then the phone call had come in, and when he'd returned to his seat it had felt to Asai as if the news were a bizarre figment of his imagination. He had not yet grasped the reality that Eiko was dead.

"Of course. I get it. You remember the owner of the cosmetics shop in Yoyogi who helped Eiko the day she died? We've had the memorial service now, so how about going and offering our thanks?"

"Good idea! I've been thinking about it for a while, but with all that's been going on, I never got around to it. I think we should take her some kind of gift."

"You know, she turned up at the funeral. She even gave us condolence money. When I opened the envelope there was five thousand yen inside. So much, even though we'd caused her nothing but trouble. I told you about the money, didn't I?"

"Yes, you did. Do you think you'd remember how to get to her shop?"

Miyako thought she could, so they set out that afternoon to visit the little cosmetics boutique in the Sanya district of Yoyogi where Eiko had collapsed and died.

3

Ever since the streets of Yoyogi had been redone for the 1964 Tokyo Olympics, the character of the area had changed completely. Still, if you got off the main roads, there was some of the old atmosphere left. Here and there you caught traces of the steep slopes that the artist Ryusei Kishida had depicted in his 1915 painting *Kiritoshi no shasei* ("Road Cut Through a Hill"). Obviously, that famous view of uneven red earth had long since become grey asphalt, and there was not a single tuft of wild grass to be seen, but long expanses of the famous stone walls had been repaired and lined both sides of the street. Luxury homes and grand apartment buildings filled the empty land beyond the walls. The desolate landscape that Kishida had fallen in love with when he first moved to Yoyogi in the early part of the twentieth century was now a prime residential zone.

Asai walked side by side with his sister-in-law along one of the main streets that intersected with the famous *kiritoshi* road. It was lined with the kind of high-end businesses popular in affluent neighbourhoods. It was a warm afternoon for mid-March, and sweat dripped down the back of his neck, dampening his winter scarf.

As they climbed the hill, there were more of these spacious family homes built on embankments above the stone walls. This area, with its larger houses, had never suffered bomb damage in the war, so a good number still remained. Dotted in between these were newer homes and apartment buildings.

Miyako was walking a step or two ahead of Asai, carrying a fruit basket over her arm.

"It's a very tiny boutique, hidden away all by itself, right in the middle of all these private homes," she called back to him. "It's hard to remember exactly where – I only came here the once. I remember there was a house with a massive zelkova tree in the front garden right next to it… Oh, there it is!"

Asai followed Miyako's gaze. At the next bend in the road he could see a tall zelkova; its tip and branches had a light dusting of new, green shoots.

As they rounded the bend, the house with the zelkova came into full view. Its low stone wall was topped with a tall bamboo fence stretching for about a hundred and twenty yards. Along the base of the fence was an azalea hedge, and above, the heads of several evergreen trees poked out from inside the garden. The zelkova tree was right in the corner. At the bottom of a flight of stone steps leading down from the house was a roofed gateway. The nameplate on the gate read KUBO. The nameplate, the gate, the bamboo fence and the partially visible two-storey house were all very old. It was fairly typical of the homes in this neighbourhood.

Miyako stopped just beyond the Kubo house. The frontage of the next building was only about three or four yards wide; the second floor was almost completely hidden by a large sign that read TAKAHASHI COSMETICS. It was a small shop, but the products displayed in the window were colourfully packaged and the whole place gave off a cheerful vibe.

"This is it," Miyako announced, taking off her light-grey coat. Underneath, her suit was the exact same shade.

On the other side of the boutique, built on an incline, was a western-style house with its own garage. It looked brand new. There was a front lawn surrounded by stylish iron railings. In the middle of the lawn was a traditional Japanese rock garden. Glancing at the nameplate, Asai could read the name HORI.

Asai removed his overcoat as well, and followed Miyako into the boutique. The interior was narrow, and it was a little awkward for two people to stand side by side.

A round-faced woman of thirty-seven or thirty-eight, dressed in a white work coat, appeared from the back of the shop. She initially registered surprise when she saw Miyako, but swiftly turned this into a smile. Her eyes were big and her lips full, and her complexion was made up to look as white as possible, as if she were modelling her own cosmetics range. She was on the short side, but had a full, shapely figure.

"Thank you for all you did for my sister... And thank you so much for coming to the funeral service. We truly appreciated your offering."

Miyako suddenly remembered that she was accompanied by the husband of the deceased.

"This is my sister's husband. I'm sorry that we've left it so long, but we're here to thank you for your kindness."

Miyako took a step or two backwards, and Asai stepped forward.

"I'm Tsuneo Asai," he said, holding out his name card and bowing deeply. "I'm truly sorry for all the trouble my wife caused you. There really isn't any good way to apologize. I should have visited you earlier to express my apologies and my thanks for all you did for her, but her passing was so sudden, and I was so busy taking care of the funeral arrangements. Then it wasn't possible to visit until after the seventh-day memorial service, so I'm afraid I'm rather late to offer my thanks."

"I'm so sorry for your loss. Has the seventh-day memorial really taken place already? It all feels like a dream to me – I can't imagine what it must be like for you."

Following this appropriate exchange of greetings, Asai placed the basket of fruit on the glass-topped counter, along with an envelope containing three 10,000-yen notes.

The boutique owner seemed flustered. "You really didn't need to do that," she said, hurriedly pushing the envelope back towards Asai.

"No, we insist. It's an expression of our regret. We feel terrible for all the inconvenience you've suffered. Please accept this small gift."

Miyako joined him in a deep bow, but the shopkeeper was unmoved.

"No, truly. I only did what anyone would have done. But I couldn't even save her. I wish things had turned out differently. It was so tragic."

"No, really, it's no more than we owe you. We realize that you had to shut up shop that day while you dealt with my sister and waited for the car to come."

"No, no. I'm really not all that busy here. I only had to draw the curtains at the front for a couple of hours. It didn't have that much effect on business at all."

It suddenly seemed to occur to her that she wasn't being polite.

"I'm so sorry to keep you standing all this time. My shop's only small, but you're more than welcome to come and sit back here."

She directed them to the back of the boutique. Miyako picked up the money envelope from the counter and took it with her.

There were several showcases filled with cosmetics, which acted as a kind of divider, blocking the view of the back from the main part of the shop. Tucked away behind them was a small table with four chairs. It was dark back there with the display cases blocking the light from the front of the store, but the shopkeeper turned on an overhead light.

It would have been proper for Asai to leave after exchanging greetings with the shopkeeper, but he was anxious to hear more details of how Eiko had ended up in that boutique, and about the moment she'd drawn her very last breath, so he went ahead and took a seat next to Miyako. He'd heard the whole story from his sister-in-law, more or less, but now he wanted to hear a first-hand account. That, and he needed to pay his respects to the woman who had helped his wife in her final moments.

The shopkeeper disappeared for a few minutes, most likely preparing some tea for her guests. There was no sign of any other family members around. Nor did the boutique seem to have any employees besides the owner; the business was probably too small to be able to afford any sales staff. However, thanks to its location it was offering some very expensive designer items. Asai pondered this as his eye was caught by a poster advertising a famous line of cosmetics.

The proprietor, still in her white coat, returned with three cups of black tea on a silver tray.

"Thank you. You needn't have gone to so much trouble," murmured Miyako, rising slightly from her chair to bow.

"No, no trouble at all. I'm sorry it's not much," replied the shopkeeper, placing a cup of tea in front of Asai. Then she produced her name card. In the top right-hand corner were the names of two famous cosmetics companies with whom she evidently had a special contract. The middle line read TAKAHASHI COSMETICS, and on the left her name, Chiyoko Takahashi, followed by her address and telephone number in fine print. There was no mention of other family members.

Ms Takahashi politely read Asai's name card before placing it on the table in front of her. She must have noted the title "Second Section Chief" in the Department of Staple Foods at the Ministry of Agriculture and Forestry, but she said nothing, and her face betrayed no emotion. Asai added some sugar to his tea and used the back of his teaspoon to squeeze the floating lemon slice against the bottom of his teacup. He took a sip and began to speak.

"I've heard the basic version from my sister-in-law here, but I'd really appreciate it if you could tell me more about how my wife ended up in your shop and what you did for her."

"Of course. It wouldn't be respectful to your late wife if I didn't tell her husband the whole story."

Chiyoko Takahashi leaned her head back slightly and began. Asai noticed her mouth. Her lips were extremely prominent, but her make-up was so adeptly applied that it was hardly noticeable; in fact, they even added to her attractiveness.

"It was the seventh of March, a Friday, around four in the afternoon. I was here in the back when your wife suddenly appeared in the shop. I assumed she was a customer, so I called out '*Irrashaimase* – welcome!' I walked over – she was standing in front of the glass showcase, right about where you were standing earlier, not speaking. I asked her if there was something she'd like me to show her, but she just stood there in silence. I think she was trying so hard to control the pain from the heart attack that her mouth just wouldn't move. She'd been walking along the street —"

"I'm sorry, but which direction did she come from?"

Asai's unexpected interruption appeared to throw Ms Takahashi for a moment, but she quickly recovered.

"She came from the left," she said, pointing out towards the street. It was the same direction from which Asai and Miyako had come. It was an uphill climb, but not a particularly steep one. Steep hills were doubtlessly not good for people with weak hearts, Asai thought, but this slope couldn't possibly have been the cause. Eiko had just happened to be walking up this street when she was taken ill.

"I see. I'm so sorry I interrupted you." Asai nodded at Chiyoko Takahashi to encourage her to continue.

"As your wife was walking up the hill, she suddenly began to feel ill. However, any woman would feel awkward collapsing outside in the street; it would be undignified to end up lying out there on the ground. So I think she desperately tried to control the pain until she could somehow make her way into a shop, and mine was the first she saw. As you probably noticed, most of the buildings around here are rather fine family homes. Mine is the only business. And I suppose the fact that it was a cosmetics boutique made it a little easier for your wife to enter. She probably just hurried in as fast as she could."

That was true. In a crisis, any shop would have done, but Asai was sure that one that catered exclusively to women would have been more comfortable for Eiko.

"I noticed there was something wrong with your wife, and I asked her what the matter was. I went over to her, and she held up her handbag as if she were trying to get me to take it. I realized she wanted me to open it up and find her ID so I could call someone for her. And when I eventually did, I came across her appointment book. Her name and address were written in it."

That was Eiko's haiku notebook. Ever since taking up haiku, she never left home without it in her handbag. When they'd brought her body home, her father had passed the handbag over to Asai and he'd seen the book inside.

"But I'm afraid I didn't realize what she meant right away. I was too worried about her. She suddenly crouched down with both hands pressed to her chest. I was busy trying to support her from behind. I guess I was in kind of a panic."

Miyako had her handkerchief out, and was dabbing at her eyes.

"I saw your wife's face was deathly pale, so I did my best to support her weight and get her into the back of the boutique. My sitting room is through there – it's a tatami mat room – so I took her in there, but by then she had completely collapsed and seemed to be in great distress. I was all alone, and I had no idea what to do. And right at that moment, a young university student who lives in the neighbourhood turned up to buy some make-up. Doctor Ohama has a clinic about five doors up, off to the right – I got her to run over and ask him for help."

The rest of the story was just as Asai had heard from Miyako. Doctor Ohama had rushed straight over, but by the time he got there Eiko had already stopped breathing. Looking for something to identify the woman who had stumbled into her shop, Chiyoko Takahashi had opened Eiko's handbag and found her appointment book. Her name and address were written there, but unfortunately no telephone number. Nor was there any entry in the telephone directory under "Eiko Asai"; the entry would of course have been under her husband's name.

One way to find the number would have been to go through all the many Asais in the phone book one by one, checking the addresses, but in her distress it hadn't occurred to the cosmetics shop owner to try.

Looking through the diary, she'd eventually found someone else's name and number, and called it. It had turned out to be Eiko's haiku teacher, who lived in Horinouchi, Suginami Ward. The teacher in turn had called Eiko's home, where Miyako had answered. This was why it had taken so long for Asai to hear.

In all, Ms Takahashi's story took about forty minutes to tell, and by the end Asai felt that he had a clearer picture of the circumstances of Eiko's death.

"The more I hear, the more I realize how much we owe you," said Asai, bowing once more. "Unfortunately,

I happened to be on a business trip in Kobe when it happened."

"Yes, very unfortunate. It must have been an awful shock when you heard the news."

"Well, yes, it was."

"Yes, and so suddenly, on top of that. May I ask, was your wife in poor health before it happened?"

"I'm not sure that I'd say poor health exactly. She'd had symptoms previously, but extremely mild ones. She really didn't have any problems in her day-to-day life. I mean, she got around just fine."

"That really is too bad."

At this point, Miyako once again offered the envelope with the thank-you money. The little dance between Ms Takahashi and Asai was repeated until finally the shop-keeper accepted the gift.

"I appreciate it very much," she said, bowing deeply.

During this whole time, not a single customer had entered the boutique, nor did there appear to be anyone else in the living quarters. When she said that she had been alone the day Eiko had run into her shop, and hadn't known what to do, eventually sending a young student to fetch the doctor, Asai believed it. He guessed that she was always there by herself. Miyako had also mentioned that when she and her father had arrived by car to pick up Eiko's body, there had been no sign of anyone else around.

Asai picked up his coat and made to leave. Ms Takahashi politely stopped him and helped him put it on. He caught a waft of expensive perfume when she approached him; apparently another tool of the trade.

"The houses around here are impressive," he remarked, averting his gaze from Ms Takahashi's dark, round eyes.

"Yes, my boutique is the only small place around."

Chiyoko Takahashi smiled for the first time since they'd met. Under the heavy, whitish make-up Asai could see a whole web of crow's feet.

"I noticed you've got all the top brands. I guess they're the kind of thing popular with the people around here," remarked Miyako.

"Yes, that's right. Or at least that was the plan."

Pleasantries were exchanged one last time, and Asai and Miyako left. Asai set off up the hill. His sister-in-law called after him.

"Hey, Tsuneo-san, that's the wrong way!"

"I know, but I thought I'd check out this road a little more. Have a look at all the gorgeous houses."

Asai felt that it would be soothing to his soul to wander around this quiet part of the city and enjoy the view of all the elegant homes. He persuaded Miyako to join him for a short walk.

Next to Chiyoko Takahashi's boutique was the house with the name HORI marked on the gate. Beyond that, a traditional Japanese-style house which belonged to ISHIDA, with a pine tree in the front garden. Across the street, the tips of a bamboo hedge were visible above a concrete wall. The nameplate on the gate read KOBAYASHI.

As he walked, Asai lifted his gaze towards the top of the hill. Way up above him he could see a neon sign. It read HOTEL TACHIBANA.

4

As he walked up the hill with Miyako, Asai began to wonder. On the day she died, what had brought Eiko to this street? He'd never heard her mention the neighbourhood to him, ever.

He had of course asked Miyako the same question the moment he arrived home from Kobe the morning after Eiko's death. But she'd had no answer.

"Me? I've no idea what she was doing there. I assumed you'd know."

"No, she never mentioned it to me. You were there when she left the house, weren't you? Didn't she say where she was going?"

"Not specifically. She said she was going to the Ginza area to do some shopping, then calling in on someone on the way back. She didn't tell me any more than that, and I didn't bother to ask."

"Eiko must have known someone up Yoyogi way. I've heard quite a bit about her friends from school, but I didn't think any of them lived around there."

"It must have been one her haiku friends, then. She must have been on her way to their house. Or perhaps coming back."

"Maybe," said Asai, still unconvinced. "She hasn't been

doing haiku for all that long, so I don't know anyone from that group of friends."

"Why don't I ask her haiku teacher? I think she's coming to the wake."

Eiko's haiku teacher had indeed turned up to the wake, along with five or six of Eiko's fellow pupils. She was an elegant, full-figured lady with a striking head of silver hair. It had been the first time Asai had met her, and he'd been struck by her slightly husky voice.

"Aoki-sensei says she doesn't have any pupils who live in Yoyogi," Miyako informed Asai, after the teacher had left. "Maybe Eiko wasn't heading to Yoyogi at all, but just happened to pass through on her way to somewhere else."

Miyako didn't seem particularly interested in why her sister had been in that part of town. She was probably right – Eiko must have simply been passing through.

Eiko had used to go out about twice a week, and, occasionally, if it had been a while, two days in a row. Mostly it had been related to her haiku lessons, so she'd rarely gone out in the evening – it was almost always in the daytime, when Asai was at work.

When Asai got home at night, Eiko would often tell him about her day. It wasn't anything terribly interesting – haiku wasn't really Asai's thing – so he'd never listened all that carefully. It had been the same when she'd been studying traditional ballads or Japanese painting. It wasn't his own hobby, so he'd been indifferent. Besides, she'd only been out of the house for three or four hours at a time and had always been back before Asai.

But now, as he left Takahashi Cosmetics and turned to climb the steep slope, the need to know why Eiko had been walking up that very hill was suddenly overwhelming. Now that he was here in person, his mind was filled with misgivings.

The road was lined with large houses; some old and some new. There were no other little shops like Takahashi Cosmetics – except one, which sold milk products.

Eiko had been walking up this hill, in the same direction that he and Miyako were going now. He stared at the road ahead of him, the asphalt dazzling in the sunshine. His sister-in-law was a short distance behind him.

Right where the road curved to the left they arrived at the highest point; beyond that, there was a steep drop. The houses below were much smaller, and from up here they seemed to tumble away together down the hill, roof after roof basking in the warm sunshine. Behind one of the fences, Asai could see a lone, scraggy peach tree, half-heartedly blooming. As they walked, the road continued to slope up and down.

At the top of the next incline there was a side street. The building on the right-hand corner was the Hotel Tachibana, which Asai had seen from further down the hill. Viewed in broad daylight, the heavy neon sign, with its rusting frame, sat forlornly on the roof.

A long concrete wall ran along the front of the hotel, with a thick row of evergreens beyond. There were also some late plum blossoms dotted in between. Asai could see a two-storey Japanese-style building, and a separate four-storey western-style one next to it. The gate was set back from the road, its posts made from thick, dark cedar trunks, their bark still intact. To the immediate right and left of the gate, the concrete wall briefly gave way to a bamboo fence. A path of stepping stones led away from the gate, set in a landscape of tiny black pebbles and lined by azaleas. The stepping stones were illuminated by a line of stone lanterns. Thick bamboo foliage concealed the entranceway to the building. Both the buildings and the garden had been designed to give the illusion of high-end elegance. A little further down there was a gap in the wall serving as a car-park entrance.

It took only a single glance for Asai to imagine the kind of clientele such a place would attract. Looking down the road to the right, it was hard to miss a second building sporting a large neon sign – this time the symbol for a hot-spring bathhouse.

Asai wondered what kind of street he'd stumbled upon, and turned to look behind him. Miyako was walking a good distance behind, her eyes fixed on the ground, perhaps because she too had spotted the dubious hotel. Asai was about to call out to her, but hesitated and instead turned right onto the little side street, heading downhill.

He heard the sound of a car behind him. The street was narrow as well as steep, forcing Asai and Miyako to stop and move as far to the side of the road as possible. A white, medium-sized saloon passed them. In the driver's seat was a middle-aged man wearing a leather jacket; in the passenger seat, a young woman in a red coat. The woman had one arm around the man's shoulder. Asai pictured the car park entrance at the Tachibana.

On Monday morning, Asai happened to be walking down one of the ministry's corridors, about to deliver some documents, when he met Director-General Shiraishi coming from the opposite direction. They were right in front of the minister's secretariat, but today there were hardly any petitioners from the business sector. The whole floor seemed to be deserted.

Asai halted and waited for Shiraishi to notice him. The heavily built figure approached, and stopped in front of him.

"Hello there!" Mr Shiraishi looked sympathetically at Asai. "I'm sorry. You must be feeling awfully lonely these days."

Mr Shiraishi had visited Asai to offer his condolences. As soon as the customary forty-nine days had passed, Asai intended to return the call and offer the appropriate thank-you gift. On his very first day back at work after the funeral, he had already made sure to pay a call to the director general's office and thank him for his kindness.

"Well, it was rather sudden, so I suppose I'm still finding it hard to take in."

"Yes, I suppose so... I can see that it would be."

It was clear that the director general had some kind of pressing business. In fact, the expression on his face suggested that he had run into Asai at an inopportune moment. But given the nature of the conversation, a few casual words in passing wouldn't have been enough. He'd been forced to stop and talk, and now he couldn't escape.

"I must thank you, sir, for all your thoughtfulness. I'm so sorry for all the trouble I've caused you... Well, please don't let me keep you."

Asai bowed deeply.

"Yes, well, er… keep your chin up."

"Thank you, sir."

The director general strode away.

When he guessed Shiraishi was a fair distance away, Asai turned to look. His manager was standing in front of the lifts, staring at the floor indicator. When he was all by himself, he looked like a complete nobody. Among a crowd of his subordinates or hangers-on, he had the air of the consummate director general. Clearly he was good at faking it. Next to the undersecretary, in the presence of the Cabinet Minister himself, or when he was alone he looked helpless, definitely not someone you could depend on – in fact, no different from one of the guards who stood at the ministry's main entrance. In other words, anyone could have done his job. It seemed all that was necessary was to graduate from an elite university and to get placed on the elite track along with all your fellow chosen ones; all destined to be future top executives. After that, all you had to do was to successfully ride that wave between the mainstream and other political currents, and you had it made.

Asai had been back in his office about an hour when someone came up beside his desk and gave a quick bow. Looking up, he saw Mr Yagishita from the Kobe Food Manufacturers' Association.

"Good morning, Mr Asai."

Yagishita's expression was unusually humble. It was probably because this was the first time he had seen Asai since his business trip to Kobe, and he wanted to express his condolences. Asai swivelled around in his chair.

"Hello. When did you get here?"

For some reason, Asai pictured Director-General Shiraishi's face as he spoke.

"Just this morning, around eleven." Yagishita then proceeded to offer Asai the traditional phrases of condolence in his Kansai regional dialect. When he'd finished speaking, Asai responded in the appropriate manner.

"Thank you. You really were a great help to me… Er, Mr Yagishita, do you have time right now? I'd like to grab a cup of tea downstairs."

"If you're not too busy, I'd be happy to join you."

They headed to the staff canteen in the basement. It wasn't quite lunchtime, so there were very few ministry employees around. However, at a few of the tables there were groups of manufacturers or traders sitting with the member of staff handling their case.

Before taking his seat, Yagishita placed both hands on the table and bowed his head once more.

"Once again, I'm so sorry for your unexpected tragedy."

"I'm ever so grateful that you took so much trouble to pay your respects."

Yagishita had sent his firm's Tokyo business manager to attend Eiko's wake and funeral on his behalf. And he'd contributed a very generous 50,000 yen in condolence money.

"Oh, you're welcome. I really should have come up myself, but you know how swamped it can get at work. Anyway, I'm here today for all the preparations we have left to get the new Kanto area factory up and running. I'm so sorry to bother you with all my own stuff."

"That's all right. How's it going out at Higashi Murayama? Is the plant in operation yet?"

"Yes, I'm glad to say. Thanks to all your help, we've somehow managed to get it going."

Yagishita had recently acquired a small ham-processing plant out to the west of Tokyo and remodelled the whole facility, establishing a Tokyo branch of the Yagishita Ham Manufacturing Corporation. Asai had been involved in the approval process.

"We've finished installing the new machinery and expanding the facilities. It all passed inspection, so we're going to begin operations three days from now."

"Congratulations! How many employees do you have?"

"About ten people have come up from Osaka, and we've taken on about twenty from the staff of the old place. Now we're busy filling all the rest of the vacancies."

"You're quite the old pro, aren't you?"

"Thanks for the compliment. As you know, competition in the industry is pretty fierce. There's no knowing how the Tokyo expansion is going to turn out."

"So are you busy this evening?"

"Ah, I, um, already made plans," Yagishita replied, a little uncomfortably. Once again the image of Director-General Shiraishi standing by the elevators popped into Asai's head.

"I see," he said, carefully stirring his coffee. "By the way, thank you for helping me out back in Kobe. How did it go after that?"

"After you left? Well, there was quite a commotion." As he recounted the story, Yagishita became very animated. "When everyone heard that your wife had passed away, they were floored. They all said it was typical of you not to make a fuss and to leave so discreetly. 'That's just like Mr Asai,' they said. They were full of admiration."

"Thank you; it was nothing. Simply the right thing to do in the circumstances."

Asai took a sip of coffee before continuing.

"But that wasn't what I meant." He adjusted the tone and level of his voice. "I asked you to *look after* Shiraishi for me. I just wanted to know that everything went off without a hitch."

"Oh, you mean *that*?"

Yagishita gave Asai a meaningful look and stuck out his little finger in the gesture for "girlfriend". "Yes, that went very well," he said, grinning.

Asai remembered the round-cheeked geisha from the drinks party. The way that Yagishita had confidently assured him that he could take care of the director general suggested that she must have been a woman of rather loose morals, but in Asai's opinion she was still much too good for Shiraishi.

"Mr Asai?"

Yagishita interrupted Asai's musings.

"Does Director-General Shiraishi have any plans for another trip to Kansai?" he asked, grinning.

"No, I've not heard of any. He's only just got back from the last one."

Asai had answered unthinkingly, but then he caught something in Yagishita's expression.

"You heard something from him directly, huh?"

"No, no. Mr Shiraishi didn't say anything specifically – it was just my own guess."

"He really liked Kobe, did he?"

Yagishita grinned some more. "Well, yes. So it seems. And for us manufacturers it'd be an honour to have the director general visit regularly."

"I suppose it'd be possible. Then you'll need to start working on an invitation to Mr Shiraishi – invite him to conduct another inspection tour of the Kansai region or something."

Yagishita's smile was blinding.

"Obviously we'll make all the necessary arrangements at our end, but that's not going to be enough to get the director general to go for it. That part's going to be up to you, Mr Asai. If you could lay all the proper groundwork…"

"I suppose if he's already amenable to the idea, then I could sort something out."

"Do you think you'd be able to accompany him again?"

"Me? I don't think so. It was my turn last time. It's bound to be someone else the next time. There are other section chiefs, you know. And then there are assistant division chiefs, division chiefs and so on… There's no shortage of qualified people."

"I'll make sure that the manufacturers' association puts in a request for you to come too. And I think it's good for Mr Shiraishi to have someone he already knows. I mean, you'd been right there by his side the whole time up until that dinner party. And besides, I gave him the heads-up that we were the ones who arranged that geisha for him."

Asai grimaced. "You told him about that?"

"If I hadn't told him, he would have hesitated to go with her."

"You think so?"

"Of course. And hearing that, he knows you were taking good care of him. I'm sure he sees you in a more favourable light now."

"Thanks for looking out for me."

"So next time Mr Shiraishi needs to appoint himself an assistant, he'll think of you straight away. I'll set it up with the manufacturers' association."

Before Asai could reply, Yagishita's balding forehead leaned in closer.

"Mr Asai, why don't you visit Kobe for a bit of fun? I'm sorry if it's inappropriate to make that kind of suggestion right after your wife has passed away."

Asai didn't know what to say.

"These kinds of trips don't come along every day. And last time you had to leave before things really got interesting. That was such a pity."

"I'll think about it."

"Here everyone's watching you, but down in Kobe you'll be away from prying eyes. And it's not as if you sleep with a woman at the restaurant or your own hotel; you go by car to an out-of-the-way place – an inn or a couples' hotel. Then no one's around to see you."

"Are there a lot of hotels like that in Kobe?"

"Sure. There are plenty of quiet places around Suma or Akashi. It's handy – you can even rent a room in the daytime."

"Do you go to places like that?"

"No. Me, I only do it at night."

Asai couldn't look at Yagishita's laughing face without seeing the gateway to the Hotel Tachibana.

5

It wasn't Yagishita's description of the couples' hotels near Kobe that put the idea into Asai's head. Since Eiko's death, there had been the little germ of an idea attached to the inner wall of his brain. Ever since he had seen the Tachibana's neon sign on top of that hill in Yoyogi, the germ had detached itself and begun to spawn, the black specks swirling around his brain and finally coming to rest right behind his eyes. These shadows blocked all outside light. The moment he heard Yagishita's story, they began to crawl over his eyes like squirming black insects, and he was spurred into action.

Eiko's weak heart had barely caused her any problems in her day-to-day life. As long as she didn't overexert herself, there were no noticeable symptoms, and she had been able to forget there was anything wrong with her at all. Still, she'd taken it upon herself to be careful not to break into a run, pick up very heavy objects, or to get upset enough to fly into a rage. She was afraid that if she had an unexpected traumatic experience or heard shocking news, or even resumed her sex life, any of these might have caused her to have a heart attack.

The road in Yoyogi was an uphill slope, and Eiko had hated walking uphill. Asai knew this, and knew it had been one of her ways of protecting her heart. So why had she been there? The proprietor of Takahashi Cosmetics had been certain that she had been heading in that direction when she'd staggered into the shop, her face white as a sheet.

Normally, Eiko would have talked to him about all of her outings, but she'd never mentioned that part of the city. So perhaps that day had been the first time she'd ever been there. Or she'd been there before but purposely not told him about it.

If Eiko had been trying to hide something, it might explain why she'd been walking up that street. At the top sat the Hotel Tachibana, with the neon sign on its roof. If she'd been heading there, she would have had to take that route – the kind of uphill road that she normally avoided. There was no other way up to the hotel.

Eiko's trips had lasted three to four hours, and had taken place in the middle of the day. Sometimes twice, sometimes three times a week. Not all these trips were to her haiku teacher's home in Suginami Ward. She'd told Asai that sometimes she visited friends and acquaintances from her haiku circle, and occasionally she would go for a stroll somewhere that might inspire a poem. Asai had heard this so many times that he'd let the information wash over him. Now he realized that he should have listened more carefully; three to four hours was just about the perfect length of time to meet a lover.

When the insects had begun to swarm, he'd grabbed Eiko's haiku notebook in an attempt to discover some written clue, but there was nothing that suggested a love affair. This was the very same notebook that Eiko had been carrying in her handbag at the time of her death; the one she'd desperately tried to show to Chiyoko Takahashi.

The notebook contained a list of addresses; a list that the haiku teacher had collected and distributed as a way of identifying all her students. There was nothing suspicious about it at all. There wasn't a single sentence written in the whole book that could be interpreted as a message of love. Eiko's own poems were in the style of the Hototogisu School of haiku, relating to the beauty of nature and the harmony between man and the natural world. Every poem was about nature. And yet not one of the locations described seemed to evoke Yoyogi. Maybe somewhere, buried deep in these poems, was a secret.

Even if Asai was on the right track, he had absolutely no idea who the lover could be. What kind of man could make Eiko burn with such desire that she forgot about her weak heart? In the whole seven years that Asai had been married to her, he'd never once seen Eiko show any interest in other men. She'd always seemed to him to have a rather bland personality – she despised romantic novels and never read them, and he'd never heard her discuss love or sex. If there was any hint of a love scene on a TV programme she would immediately change channels or turn it off.

Similarly, Eiko had shown no interest in her husband's job. She'd never made an effort to understand what kind of work he did, and never asked questions about it. She'd wanted to hear how many days he'd be away on his business trips, but never asked where he was going, who he was going with, or the purpose of the trip. She had simply checked what day he'd be home so she could get the house ready for his return. She'd been so indifferent that it didn't matter how late he came home on any given working day, she'd never bothered to ask him where he'd been.

Eiko had never been fond of spending time with the wives of his colleagues at the ministry. Asai understood it could be tedious, but all the other wives put up with it, didn't they? Surely that was their contribution to their husbands' careers. She really ought to have made more of an effort to cosy up to the wives of his superiors, but she'd never even tried. That was the kind of person Eiko had been: completely unconcerned with Asai's career advancement.

Generally, when a wife is completely disinterested in her husband's social standing, he is forced to dig deep and find his own source of motivation. This depends, of course, on the personality of the husband in question, but Asai believed he had what it took. Because he'd never enjoyed the cooperation and support of his wife, Asai knew that he'd been given the opportunity to pour all his energy into his work. If things had been different, and Eiko had been too involved in his career – if she either henpecked or overprotected him – it would have weakened his own motivation. Asai saw plenty of men like that around the ministry.

A wife who was passionately involved in her husband's career didn't necessarily love her husband any better than a wife who had no interest in it at all. Every woman was different. Actions did not necessarily speak louder than words. After seven years of marriage Asai and Eiko had a relationship as natural as air or water. Even the wives who had the deepest involvement in their husbands' careers would never have a complete understanding of their jobs. That was how Asai had always seen it.

But the wife who felt that all passion was gone from her daily life, who looked for a way to rekindle that passion with some other man besides her husband... well, he'd read about this kind of thing in novels and the advice column in the newspaper, but he'd never imagined it actually happening to him.

And yet something occurred to him when he really thought about it. Perhaps he had adjusted his own personality too easily to Eiko's. If he'd paid her a little more attention, maybe she would have been less passive. Her sensuality may have been right there under the surface waiting to blossom. But he'd been lacking as a partner. He'd been too concerned with her health problems, held back too much. The doctor had emphasized that all his warnings were just standard textbook, so there must have been some other way to continue making love. Perhaps they should have gone to other doctors, asked for more advice.

Eiko had never been assertive and definitely hadn't been the type to take the initiative in the bedroom. It seemed that she'd been unable to break the habits they'd fallen into at the start of their marriage. Perhaps she didn't have the courage. The rigidity of their seven years of marital relations had gradually formed a protective shell into which she had retreated.

This other man would have had to work on breaking that shell and overcoming the modesty that she had always shown around her husband. And it looked as if he had found a way in. She had apparently undergone a complete transformation.

Asai recalled something the doctor had said, way back.

"Heart disease is an invisible illness, undetectable in everyday life, so people tend to become careless. Let me give you an example. One of my friends, a doctor who suffers from heart disease himself, was out one day driving his car to a house call when his tyre got stuck in the drainage ditch by the side of the road. He got out, tried to lift the car out of the ditch, and instantly suffered a heart attack. He died on the spot. Even though he was a doctor, he completely forgot about his own illness. You need to take care."

Who was this object of Eiko's obsession? Who had made her forget about her disease? This man who had given her a shock strong enough to paralyse her coronary artery – where was he?

It struck Asai now that the reason Eiko never read romantic fiction or watched soap operas or other TV dramas wasn't because she'd disliked them. She'd been avoiding them. She didn't want to stir up all those feelings and sensations that she'd been trying to repress. And he'd taken it for a lack of interest!

Eiko had studied singing and painting, so she must have had a sensitive side. She'd been interested in romance novels and TV soaps after all. She avoided them so that they wouldn't awaken her sexual desire. Taking singing then giving it up, switching to painting and giving that up too, never sticking with anything for long – she was seeking something elusive, something that she needed. Did those ballads stir something tremendous in her soul? Traditional Japanese-style painting was probably far too tame. But in order to express the true beauty of nature in a haiku poem, she needed to go outside, take walks: that was when the opportunity had presented itself.

Yes, her lover was someone she'd met since taking up haiku. Sometime in the past couple of years, not before.

But here was the mystery: why had Eiko been *walking* up that hill? In other words, why hadn't she been in a taxi or some other vehicle? All the other people that he and Miyako had seen that Sunday – the couple leaving the hotel and others who looked as if they were on their way in – had all been in cars. It was the natural way to travel when you were going to a place like that. No one wanted to show their face – best to simply drive in.

What's more, Eiko hated steep hills. It wasn't like her to walk when she could have been driven. So why had she been on foot?

Asai spent the next few days mulling over this puzzle, not only at home in his spare time but at work too. He checked over documents, drafted proposals, issued orders to his junior staff, consulted with his senior managers, met with visiting manufacturers, attended meetings and coordinated with staff in other departments, all the while absorbed by this conundrum.

Eventually all the little threads of ideas and conjecture came together in his mind and formed a viable hypothesis...

Eiko had suffered a heart attack while she was at a hotel with her lover. How should the man have reacted? Normally, he would have called a doctor, but this hotel was decidedly dodgy. It would have been impossible to remain anonymous. A heart attack was serious. You couldn't get away with giving a false name.

The man must have decided he had to get out of the hotel before calling for help. He got the hotel to call a taxi, and somehow got Eiko into it. Unfortunately, the pain had got worse, and he'd let her out of the taxi somewhere down the hill – probably near the bottom, a little way beyond Takahashi Cosmetics. That would explain why Chiyoko Takahashi had seen her come up the hill from the left.

How could Eiko's lover have made her get out of the taxi like that? Maybe he was taken by surprise by the seriousness of her condition; maybe he realized she needed the attention of a doctor right away. But why didn't he drop her in front of a hospital, then? Because the hospital would have questioned the identity of a man who turned up with a half-dead woman in his arms. After arriving like that, it would have been difficult for him to make his escape. Time was running out, so the man had dropped Eiko off. He'd left her to run into the nearest house so she could get them to call an ambulance. Someone had been bound to help. He'd decided this was the best way to deal with the situation. He had never needed to give a name or address. He'd simply offloaded his problem on the side of the road and fled. Writhing in agony from the heart attack, Eiko couldn't protest.

Asai's investigation began with the Tachibana.

On his way home from work, he stopped in at an *oden* restaurant for a drink, then took a taxi up to Yoyogi. As the car drove past Takahashi Cosmetics, he peered out at the shopfront, but the brightly lit boutique was empty and there was no sign of Chiyoko Takahashi. Miyako had confessed that she was intrigued by the female shopkeeper and the fact that she seemed to be living there in that house all alone. The shop was probably empty right now because she had no family members to help out. But there were no customers either. It wasn't exactly a thriving business. Anticipating good sales from this upmarket residential neighbourhood, she'd stocked only the most expensive brands – an amateurish mistake. She was like a widow who'd tried to go it alone after the death of her husband. Miyako had assumed right away that Ms Takahashi was a widow, and that had piqued her interest even more. Asai had an uncomfortable feeling that inside his sister-in-law's head there was already a match being made between the cosmetics shop owner and himself.

The taxi sped by the family homes, which looked more sinister now in the darkness.

Asai got out right in front of the hotel. As usual, the sign on the roof was switched on; a red neon HOTEL TACHIBANA floating in the pitch-blackness of space.

He entered through the gate he'd seen the previous Sunday. Guided by the light of the stone lanterns, he made his way across the stepping stones. Once he had navigated the front garden, he expected to arrive at the hotel entrance, but all he discovered was the side of the building and more stepping stones leading off in two different directions.

As he wondered what to do, a female employee emerged from out of the shadowy building next to him. She bowed politely but at the same time eyed him a little suspiciously. After all, he had no companion with him.

"Do you have any rooms available?"

"We do. Would you prefer one in the western style, or should I show you to a Japanese room?"

"Either's fine."

"This way, please."

The maid led him along the path to the left. In the darkness, he could just make out a small thicket of bushes.

He was shown to a small Japanese room. The sleeping area was behind a sliding paper partition, decorated with a classic pattern of tiny birds and blue waves.

An *ukiyo-e* painting hung in the alcove above a small flower vase. The wall was ochre. There was a television in the corner; next to it was a phone. As Asai sat down at the red lacquered table, the maid withdrew to the doorway, knelt and placed both hands on the tatami flooring.

"Welcome to the Tachibana. Will the... er... other party be joining you later?"

"No." Asai gave a short laugh. "There's no one else. I'm on my own."

"I see."

She didn't seem particularly surprised. Apparently single men did come to this hotel. And she had already anticipated the next question.

"I'm very sorry, but we're not able to perform that kind of service. I hope you understand."

"Oh no... I think we've had a misunderstanding. That's not why I'm here. Actually, I have a small favour to ask you."

"I'm sorry?" She regarded him uncertainly.

"I'm afraid I have rather an embarrassing question to ask. Would you mind coming a little nearer?"

The woman looked to be around forty years old and was sturdily built under her purple apron. Still kneeling, she scooted a little closer to Asai.

"Thank you. I... um... well, it's a little difficult for me to say. Still, I've made up my mind to talk openly about it. You see, about two weeks ago my wife left me for another man – someone I've never met."

The woman's eyes didn't leave his face.

"Well, a little while back I found evidence that she'd been using this hotel. Actually, it was that box of matches – the ones by the ashtray over there. The other day, I found the same matches in my wife's handbag."

There was no response from the maid.

"I have two small children at home. The only reason I've swallowed my pride and come here to ask you these questions is because my kids are missing their mum. I just want to find her and bring her home. But right now I haven't a clue where she might be. To keep up appearances I don't want to get the police involved. I thought that if I came here, I might be able to find out what kind of man my wife was here with. If I just knew what he looked like I might be able to guess who he is... Oh, I was forgetting: I brought a picture of my wife with me."

The humiliated husband produced his wife's photo from his pocket, and handed it to the maid.

"I hope you'll forgive me if I don't tell you my name."

6

Asai had decided that posing as an estranged husband whose wife had walked out on him was a sure way of gaining sympathy from a woman – particularly from the maids who worked at the hotel. Every day in their jobs, they witnessed other women's sexual infidelities. He was certain that off the job they would be inclined to pity a man with a cheating wife. Asai imagined this from a psychological point of view: women like these, who had been trained to act indifferently towards openly immoral behaviour, had to be repressing all kinds of feelings. Outrage for sure, a touch of jealousy; maybe even downright hatred.

This maid was now carefully examining Eiko's photo. But there was no sign that she recognized his dead wife.

"I'm sorry. I don't remember her. Should I ask some of the other maids to take a look? I don't meet all the guests who come here."

"Of course. Yes, please could you ask them?"

The maid hesitated. She was making a show of being uncomfortable disclosing his private affairs to other people, but at the same time it was obvious that she was dying to share this with her colleagues.

"Please, go ahead. I mean, that's what I came here for in the first place – to ask people about my wife. Could you just make sure it stays within these walls?"

Asai's voice was filled with distress, but the maid reassured him.

"I understand. When you work in this business, keeping secrets is part of the job description. You've nothing to worry about."

"Then if you don't mind…"

The maid's gaze returned to the photograph. She sighed.

"My, what a beautiful wife you have."

"Really?"

Asai had never thought of Eiko as a great beauty, but the photo had captured her at her best. She looked younger than her age, fresh-faced and modern.

"She looks like the quiet type."

"I used to think she was the perfect wife."

"Clearly she fell under someone's evil spell. Otherwise she'd never have left her children like that."

"Do you think the quieter types tend to be more susceptible to that kind of temptation?"

"You might be right on that. I wouldn't say it's the rule, but we do see a lot of women like that in here."

"I know it sounds strange coming from the estranged husband, but my wife never even had male friends. I didn't think she had the slightest interest in men at all."

"Although I hate to say it, that's even more dangerous."

"Why?"

"Women who spend a lot of time in the company of men learn to express their feelings better. They're also better at seeing through all the charming things that men say, and don't tend to fall for all that rubbish. And the kind of wives who go out looking for affairs, well, that's a completely different story."

Asai was shocked into silence.

"And then the ones who don't have male friends – I mean those who don't have a good relationship with an acquaintance who also happens to be a man – tend to keep all their feelings bottled up inside, and then those feelings all come flooding out the moment the opportunity presents itself."

In other words, the maid was saying that an introverted personality, one who kept her emotions sealed up inside, would be easy prey to seduction. Asai, remembering his quiet marriage "as natural as air or water", realized that she was probably right.

"I imagine your wife was on her guard against those kinds of men," the maid added, continuing her professional observations. "But I think she let her guard down when she met this one. She'd been wary of men for so long that she didn't really know enough about them any more. She had a mental image of what a man was like, but the one she met was completely different from this, and in an unguarded moment she let him in. Men these days know all sorts of tricks to pick up women."

So, according to the maid, a man with a few tricks and a bit of knowledge could worm his way into a naive woman's affections and then demolish her defences. That was surely what had happened to Eiko. This knowledge wasn't something the maid had picked up from the pages of a women's magazine. She was relating what her own eyes saw day in, day out. Asai found himself persuaded by her argument.

"So, in your experience, what happens after a married woman falls for a man like that?" he asked.

The maid looked modestly down at the floor, but a hint of a cold smile played on her lips.

"To begin with, the woman is uncomfortable coming to a place like this with him. She's married to someone else, and I imagine she feels terribly guilty. At first she's timid and fearful, but over time she begins to get used to it and begins to relax more on her visits. By the end of it, it's the woman who has taken the lead. She becomes so brazen that at times we can hardly believe she's the same person. Her passion for the man gets obsessive. It's not unusual for them to start coming here in the middle of the day. If she's a housewife, it's easier to arrange that way."

The maid's last words really hit home. There was no hint of irony; they were plain and honest. And Asai recognized the pattern. Eiko used to go out in the daytime two or three times a week. All she had to do was be back before her husband got home from work.

"Why don't these couples go to several different hotels? The men too, but particularly the women – surely it feels weird for them to run into the same staff all the time."

"The young ones like to mix it up, but middle-aged couples don't; staying at several different hotels means they'll be seen by many more people. And that feels even more shameful."

"I see."

"And older couples are much more likely than young ones to form a kind of attachment to a particular hotel."

The maid took Eiko's picture away, leaving Asai alone in the room. While he waited for her to return, a younger maid appeared with a tray of tea and cakes. He hadn't ordered anything, but she assured him that it was on the house. He realized that his story of being abandoned by his wife had aroused sympathy among the hotel staff. He could practically hear the maids crying, "Oh the poor thing!" If he could just put up with the humiliation a little longer, it would really help his investigation.

After about forty minutes the first maid returned, accompanied by a slightly older woman dressed in the same purple apron. She introduced herself as the head housekeeper and offered her sympathies to Asai.

"I'm very sorry to hear about the situation you're in. We've shown your wife's picture to all the maids who work here, but I'm afraid that nobody recognizes her. And there are several of our staff members who never forget a face."

The first maid carefully returned Eiko's photo to Asai. He didn't think that they were lying. They'd been nothing but compassionate right from the beginning.

"I see. Then this can't be the right hotel."

In one sense, Asai was disappointed, as he'd been so sure that his hunch was correct. On the other hand, he was slightly relieved.

"You said your wife had a box of our hotel's matches, is that correct?" the head housekeeper asked him.

The matches had been a fabrication that had got Asai the information he needed. He could hardly go back and admit he'd lied.

"Now that I've looked more closely at the matches you have here, I think the box my wife had in her bag was just very similar. I never really picked them up and examined them closely. My memory is a little hazy, now that I think about it. But what I do know for certain is that an eyewitness saw her walking up the hill that leads to this place. That's what made me think that she must have been heading here."

The housekeeper and maid exchanged a look. Then the housekeeper spoke.

"We're not the only hotel on this hill; there are two more beyond us. One, the Midori, is just close by, and the other's a little further up – the Mori. But there's another, more direct route that leads to the Mori, so I'd say if your wife was seen walking up the hill, then she was probably heading to the Midori."

Asai decided now that he'd turned himself into a desperate husband whose wife had walked out on him, he might as well continue carrying her photo around other hotels, and show it to even more of their employees. He was going to have to endure further humiliation if he was going to get the information he needed.

"I'm sorry for all the trouble I've put you to," he said with feeling.

"Oh, you're welcome. I hear that you have children. I hope you all find a way to be happy again. I'm sure that your wife will return for their sake."

With these words of comfort, the housekeeper and maid showed him out.

Asai exited the Tachibana's main gate and stood for a moment at the top of the hill, looking down. The street just below him was lined on both sides by wide-roofed mansions and was completely dark. Way down below that, the lights of the bustling city stretched out before him. Everything looked peaceful from up here.

Eiko wasn't coming back. She'd been turned to ash and was waiting at the local temple for the engraver to finish her memorial stone. Then she'd be laid to rest beneath it.

Who was responsible? Where was the man whose charm had tempted her all the way to her death? And how had this man managed to get close to Eiko in the first place? Asai hadn't the faintest idea, and had no clue as to the mystery man's identity.

He kept walking southwards, up the slope. The Hotel Midori's gaudy neon sign flashed against the night sky. He imagined the flaming red lights were designed to stimulate sexual appetite, luring men and women to a den of mind-numbing pleasure.

In just five minutes Asai was at the hotel's gate. The exterior was pretty similar to that of the Tachibana, and the concept more or less the same – the tiny pebbles and the plants glowed in the darkness from the light of low stone lanterns.

While he was hesitating outside, a man and a woman hurried past him through the gate. They were young, and didn't speak as they crunched their way along the pebble path. Asai waited a couple of minutes, then followed them inside. To his left, what looked a lot like a roadside tea house was the only place that was brightly lit. From that direction he heard a woman's voice.

"*Irrashaimase* – welcome."

A maid had stepped out to greet him, and he realized at once that this must be the hotel's reception.

"Will someone be joining you later?"

The same question as at the Tachibana.

He guessed there must be about ten maids working at this hotel. Assuming there were about the same number at the previous hotel, then he'd end up showing his wife's picture to over twenty people. He could ask them to keep it among themselves, as it was such a personal matter, but he knew this would be futile. The story was going to spread. Each maid who promised faithfully to keep it secret was bound to leak it to one or two other people. As long as he didn't give his real name, then it wouldn't be too terrible if they discussed his story. But sneaking around and flashing Eiko's photo about like this was a really low thing to do. He felt wretched. And he might not have any luck at this hotel, either. If they hadn't seen her here, would he then have to move on to the next one? And then another, and another, until he'd visited all the hotels, inns and hostels in the neighbourhood?

The Midori's head housekeeper listened sympathetically to his heartbreaking tale. She took the photo, but when she still hadn't returned after forty minutes, he imagined how the conversation might be going.

"His wife ran off with another man. Left two children at home! The husband's going crazy searching for her. Wants her to come home for the sake of the kids. He's got no shame. Lost all self-respect, poor thing. Hey, this is her. He brought her photo. Wants to know if she came here with her lover. Have you seen her? It's okay if you have; just tell him. I feel sorry for him."

Each maid's expression when she was handed Eiko's picture would be slightly different, but by the end they'd all pretty much be close to pity.

When the housekeeper finally returned, she was accompanied by a younger, shorter maid who knelt nervously on the tatami behind her.

"I've asked everybody, but they all say she's never been to our hotel. No one has ever seen her here before," explained the housekeeper. She went on to emphasize that everyone who worked at the hotel had a good memory for faces. She indicated the young maid sitting behind her.

"This young woman says she's never seen your wife at the hotel, but she did see someone outside on the street who resembled the woman in the photo. Go on, Senko."

At her boss's urging, the twenty-something, red-cheeked maid shuffled a little further forward.

"I can't be absolutely sure that it was her, but she looks a lot like a lady I met about two months back who was walking up the hill. I was going downhill at the time, so we passed each other."

"Do you remember what day it was?" Asai asked.

The maid was still examining the photo as if trying to compare it to the woman in her memory.

"I don't remember the date exactly, but it was the middle of the month."

"About what time?"

"Around two in the afternoon."

"Why do you remember her so clearly?"

"Because there was hardly anyone in the street. That lady and I were the only ones around. Normally I pass lots of people when I'm walking, but it was so quiet that day. I remember thinking it felt a bit weird, and then she walked by and I had the chance to take a good look at her face."

"And she looked like my wife in the photo."

"Yes."

"Do you remember what she was wearing?"

"I think it was a beige two-piece suit. The jacket was open at the neck and I could see a maroon-coloured scarf underneath. Her handbag was made of leather – it looked like crocodile – and it was dark red."

There was no doubt about the mystery woman's identity now. That had been one of Eiko's favourite outfits. The burgundy crocodile-skin handbag had been a present from one of the businessmen he'd helped at work. He'd brought it back from a business trip to Southeast Asia.

"You say that my wife – or at least this person who most probably was my wife – was walking alone when you saw her. Are you sure there was no one with her?"

"I'm sure. There was no one else around. She was by herself."

"Whereabouts on the hill did you pass her?"

"Right where the road begins to slope upwards."

"So it was quite a way down the street, then?"

"Right."

"There's a small boutique around there, isn't there? I think it's called Takahashi Cosmetics."

The young woman seemed surprised that Asai would have heard of such a place.

"Well, yes, there is. I met her about twenty yards down from that boutique. She was heading up the hill."

7

After leaving the Midori, Asai returned to the crossroads by the Tachibana, and set off down the hill. He checked his wristwatch under a street lamp: 9.20 p.m.

To tell the truth, he really wanted to pay a visit to the Mori, but he supposed those kind of places got busy after nine o'clock, so he decided to call it a night. Visiting two hotels in one evening had been exhausting enough.

The street wasn't well lit, and he made his way down the slope by following the concrete walls and the bamboo fences perched on top of the old stone walls. Hardly any light filtered through from the houses beyond. With the exception of the hotels on the top of the hill, it seemed this residential neighbourhood went to bed early.

Asai found himself again in front of Takahashi Cosmetics. He'd expected the lights of the shop to be spilling out onto the street, but it was just as dark as its neighbours. The glass entrance door was shut and the curtains were drawn. Asai supposed it was natural that a small boutique in this neighbourhood would also shut early. He glanced up at the first floor, where the shop sign hung. Not a glimmer of light was visible through the shutters.

The maid at the Midori had been sure that she'd seen Eiko here two months ago. From the description of her clothes and handbag there was no doubt that it had been Eiko. And it made sense that she'd been out walking around two in the afternoon.

So if she'd been walking up the slope, about twenty yards below Takahashi Cosmetics, where was that exactly? Asai estimated it was a spot approximately between the house next door to Ms Takahashi's and the one next to that. Both of these houses were traditional old Japanese-style buildings with their low stone walls intact. The one directly across the street had a concrete-block wall and a pale western-style building just visible through the trees.

Asai stopped walking and turned around to look back up at the road he had just come down. He didn't deliberately look upwards, but the steep slope meant he automatically raised his eyes.

He tried to put himself in Eiko's shoes. She'd walked up the hill as far as this point. Assuming she hadn't slowed her pace at all, her destination must have been further up. Straight ahead at the top was the Hotel Tachibana; off to the right from there, the Midori; a little further on, the Mori.

So, assuming again that she'd walked straight up this hill, her destination was most likely to have been one of the hotels, but the maids at both establishments had sworn they'd never seen her. He believed that they'd been telling the truth. They'd definitely been sympathetic to the poor abandoned husband with his two motherless children.

So where? Takahashi Cosmetics, perhaps? The story was that Eiko had begun to feel unwell and staggered into the boutique, but the maid at the Midori had seen her twenty yards before she would have reached the shop; in other words, where Asai was standing right now.

Was it a coincidence? Had Eiko visited Takahashi Cosmetics in the past, not just the day she died?

Surely that was a crazy idea. And if the maid had seen Eiko a little further up the hill, one that would never have occurred to Asai. It only crossed his mind because his wife had been seen near the bottom of the hill. Another vision came to him – this time Chiyoko Takahashi's heavily made-up face with its full lips.

So, two months before her death, Eiko had been seen here on this street. Asai imagined her destination could have been the boutique, but that was pure speculation. As long as he had no definite proof that Chiyoko Takahashi and his wife had known each other, it would remain just that. It wasn't really logical to believe that Eiko had come all the way to this particular area just to buy make-up.

Asai decided to stop his enquiries for now after investigating the two hotels at the top of the hill, and returned home to his lonely, empty house. He fell quickly into a fitful sleep, still troubled by the words of the maid at the Midori.

He woke up early. The wristwatch he'd placed by his head showed just after 6 a.m. Only a single man would put his watch next to his pillow, or someone on a trip away. Every day the feeling that he'd been abandoned grew stronger and stronger; Eiko's relatives had even stopped dropping by.

Asai lay on his stomach and smoked a cigarette. When Eiko had been alive he'd never been allowed to do this kind of thing. He wondered if he should sell the house and move into an apartment. It had been his parents' home, so it was close to forty years old. The house itself wouldn't have any value, but it stood on about three and a half thousand square feet. In this part of Tokyo, land went for about 60,000 yen per square foot. He'd have enough money to buy himself a luxury apartment. But he didn't have the status to live in a place like that. Even at the division-chief level, whole families of four were making do in cheap civil-service housing. A modest apartment would suit his needs better, he thought. It'd be a while before he married again.

He finished his cigarette and went out to collect the newspaper from the letterbox. Then he got back into bed and opened the paper. There weren't many interesting articles, but, ever the civil servant, his eye was drawn to anything connected with government policy.

There was an article about the Japan Medical Association's opposition to a new plan by the Ministry of Health and Welfare. It included comments by the chairman of the association.

Doctors... Just a moment – why had he not thought of it before?

Chiyoko Takahashi had told him that after Eiko collapsed in her boutique, she'd sent a university student, a young woman who'd just come in to buy make-up, to a nearby doctor's office to get help. He recalled the words from Ms Takahashi's own, rather memorable, lips.

"Doctor Ohama has a clinic about five doors up, off to the right – I got her to run over and ask him for help."

*

In his lunch hour, Asai took a taxi to Yoyogi. On his way up the hill he glanced at Takahashi Cosmetics, but the front entrance was shut and the curtains were drawn. It looked exactly the same as the night before. It must be closed today. Maybe it was the regular day off for all the local businesses. But no – all the shops out on the main shopping street had been open. It was only the cosmetics boutique that was closed.

Asai had the driver drop him about three streets away, opposite a narrow side street. Doctor Ohama's clinic was at the far end of the street. There was no mistaking the building for anything but a private clinic.

There was nobody in the waiting room when Asai entered. A nurse opened the glass window at the reception desk and looked out at him.

"Appointments are mornings only, I'm afraid."

"I don't need a medical appointment. I'm here to enquire about a patient."

"Could I have your name, please?"

"Asai."

"Are you a relative of this other patient?"

"Yes. She was my wife."

"How can we help you?"

"I'd like to meet with the doctor in person, if possible."

"Do you have the patient's card with you?"

"The patient's deceased."

The nurse looked at Asai for a few moments, then disappeared from the window.

About ten minutes later, the fat, bespectacled doctor came out into the waiting room. He appeared to be in his forties, and his skin looked quite good for his age. He smelled faintly of whisky. He'd obviously grabbed his white coat in a hurry; the collar was still standing up. The coat made Asai think of Chiyoko Takahashi.

The doctor looked wary. He probably thought a grieving husband had come to accuse him of killing his wife.

Asai got out his business card. The doctor read his job title, but he didn't relax his guard at all. He fetched a wooden chair and placed it across from the sofa where Asai was sitting.

"Mr Asai, could you tell me when it was I saw this patient?" He was carefully polite.

"About two weeks ago. But first I must explain that she wasn't one of your patients. She suffered a heart attack when she was out walking, and ran into a shop – Takahashi Cosmetics – just down the street from here. The owner was kind enough to call you for help."

The doctor nodded in recognition.

"I thought it might be about that lady. I couldn't think of anyone else it might have been."

Asai supposed he meant that he couldn't think of any other patients he'd killed recently. Meanwhile, Doctor Ohama's expression relaxed slightly. It seemed that Ms Takahashi had been telling the truth. Ohama had been there when Eiko passed away.

"When you arrived, Doctor, was my wife already gone? I was away on a business trip in Kansai at the time, so I don't know the full details. I only heard about it third-hand, so to speak."

"You have my sympathies." The doctor bowed his head, but it was a mere formality. "When I was called to Ms Takahashi's place, an emergency case had just arrived here at the clinic, and I couldn't leave immediately. It must have been about twenty minutes before I was able to get away. I'm afraid to say by that time your wife had already passed away. Her pupils were dilated and her heart had stopped beating. There was nothing I could do."

"Wouldn't it have been possible to give her a camphor injection, or any other kind of emergency treatment?"

"Camphor?"

The doctor's expression hardened. This was probably the one he used when dealing with complaints from the angry family members of a deceased patient.

"Do you imagine that kind of treatment would be any good to a patient who's no longer alive? When I arrived, she was lying in the tatami room at the back of the shop and she was already dead."

"What time did you arrive?"

"I checked my watch. It's very important to do that. It was 4.35 in the afternoon on the seventh of March. Actually, I checked my records just before I came out to see you. She wasn't my patient, but I issued her death certificate anyway."

"I received the certificate, thank you. I'd like to ask you about the time of death shown. It says 'around 4.05 p.m.' You say you arrived at Takahashi Cosmetics at 4.35 p.m. and confirmed that she was dead. In that case, was it just your assumption that my wife had passed away thirty minutes earlier?"

"I wasn't actually witness to her moment of passing. According to Ms Takahashi, your wife had taken her last breath about thirty minutes before I arrived. So that is what I went by. That's why I didn't write '4.05 precisely'. I put 'around 4.05'."

The doctor spoke vehemently, and the expression on his face was clearly meant to emphasize that there had been no error on his part.

"I completely understand; I'm sorry if I've made you feel uncomfortable. Please don't get me wrong. I'm simply asking whether my wife's time of death was precisely 4.05 or not. For example... how shall I put it... when you examined my wife's body, did it appear to you that she had died thirty minutes previously?"

Doctor Ohama undid his white coat and produced a cigarette case from his shirt pocket.

"As I said, I was not the attending physician at the time of your wife's death. And therefore, even though I can say she had only just passed away, it's impossible for me to tell you the exact hour, minute and second of her death."

He drew on his cigarette. Asai smiled slightly, hoping to make the doctor feel less threatened.

"That's not what I'm asking. I'm asking if there was anything strange or unnatural about her having died thirty minutes before you got there."

The doctor looked offended again.

"No, there wasn't anything strange about it at all."

"I mean, what if it hadn't been thirty minutes earlier? If it had been, say, forty minutes, would you be able to make that distinction?"

"Forty minutes earlier? Hmm. I'm not sure. All I could do was trust the word of Ms Takahashi, who had been with her at the time."

"Of course; that's only natural. But in this case I'm asking if there could have been any discrepancy in what Ms Takahashi told you. In your professional opinion, that is."

"Was there anything suspicious about your wife's death?" The doctor narrowed his eyes, and looked a little cagey.

"No, nothing suspicious. My wife had a weak heart. However, it had been years since she'd suffered a heart attack. I was told that she'd had a sudden coronary walking up that hill, but I felt that her death seemed very quick."

"No, that would have been about right. Thirty minutes before I examined her; forty at the most. Probably not as long as an hour. If I had been able to get there a little quicker I might have been able to try and massage her heart. There have been cases with a heart attack where the patient's heart was restarted by massage, but I'm sorry to say in your wife's case there was no hope."

"So, doctor, what you're saying is that there's an outside chance that she died an hour before you arrived? That would only be thirty minutes earlier than the time of death you wrote on her death certificate."

"Thirty minutes earlier? Yes, well, I suppose it's possible. Definitely within an hour of her death, anyway. But that's the absolute maximum. After an hour, it becomes much easier to determine the exact time of death. The body begins to cool rapidly, and in some cases where rigor mortis sets in early, you can find it in the muscles around the jaw, but your wife wasn't in that state. And so I based the time of death on what Ms Takahashi told me. You understand there was nothing else I could have done?"

Asai nodded solemnly.

"Of course. You couldn't have done anything differently."

"If there had been anything at all suspicious, I'd have called the police and had an autopsy done. But she wasn't a patient I normally treated, and her death appeared to

be from natural causes. Though it was sudden, of course."
The doctor frowned, as if insulted that Asai was questioning his medical prowess.

"And as Ms Takahashi pointed out, this was a lady, and
she felt sorry for her having to undergo any further examination. So given that it clearly wasn't an accidental death,
I agreed, and wrote out the death certificate."

His tone was patronizing and suggested that Asai was
somehow indebted to him.

Asai bowed deeply. "Thank you for all you did for her."

Back out on the road, he lingered a while, deciding
whether to go further up or back down. In his head he
was going over the conversation he'd just had with the
doctor. The idea that the time of death could have been
thirty minutes off was nagging at his brain. In this case,
the doctor had relied on Chiyoko Takahashi's word when
making his judgement. Asai couldn't call it a mistake; it
would be more accurate to think of it as a margin of error.

If he walked uphill, he'd be able to visit the hotel he
hadn't been to yesterday. However, his interest had been
piqued by the fact that Takahashi Cosmetics had been
closed when he'd passed by in the taxi, so he started off
downhill instead.

In less than five minutes he was in front of the boutique.
The front door and the display window were blocked off
with a heavy brown curtain. He understood why the shop
might have been closed the previous evening, but he wondered why it was shut today. There was no notice in the
window. And there was no sign of the proprietor. Maybe
because she was on her own she was free to open or close
the boutique at will.

Nobody was on the street. It was a typical peaceful afternoon in a residential neighbourhood. He remembered what the young maid at Hotel Midori had said. It had been a quiet moment like this when she had passed Eiko in the street. In her story, it had been around two o'clock. It was just after one now.

Asai approached the front door of the boutique and peered in through the gap between the curtains. The opening was very small, and all he could see was the dark interior and the faint glint of metal from something in the nearest showcase. It didn't look as if Chiyoko Takahashi was there. He continued to spy, hoping to see a sign of movement inside.

Then, feeling a presence behind him, he turned away from the window. About ten yards further up the hill there was someone watching him. It was a tall man, maybe in his thirties, wearing a grey sweater and pale-coloured trousers, with a German shepherd on a lead. The man, obviously a local resident out walking his dog, was staring at him suspiciously. The light was behind the man, so Asai couldn't make out his features; all he could tell was that he had a long face and wore glasses.

Afraid that he would be mistaken for a prowler or a thief checking out a target, Asai moved ever so casually away from the door.

8

All of Asai's investigations after that came to nothing. He took Eiko's photo to the Hotel Mori, but no one remembered having seen her. He even visited one other place, a small, Japanese-style inn a little further off the route, but again, no luck.

On his way up and back down the hill he checked out Takahashi Cosmetics. This time the boutique was open. He could see Chiyoko Takahashi in her white coat, but he wasn't brave enough to go inside. He didn't have any excuse to talk to her; they weren't on close enough terms for him to say he'd just dropped by because he happened to be in the neighbourhood. And he certainly couldn't pretend he was there to buy make-up. The only reason he could possibly be there was that he was obsessively attached to any trace of his dead wife.

As time passed, the story he'd heard from the maid began to seem less real to him. Taken out of context, it was no proof of anything. After all, the young woman didn't know Eiko; the two had never even spoken. Having a good memory didn't mean she couldn't have been mistaken about the identity of the woman in the photograph. After all, that day was probably the first time Eiko had been on the premises of the cosmetics boutique.

Although he hadn't given up all hope, Asai decided for now to forget about the hill and everything that was on it. Maybe something would pop up again sometime in the future that offered a clue to what had happened to Eiko. He just had to be patient. There was no point in rushing things. Just like at work – sometimes if he simply waited and didn't go chasing after solutions to the most challenging problems, they'd come to him of their own accord.

And anyway, he had his job. He really didn't have time to investigate all the circumstances of his wife's death. And it was exhausting to keep going back to it a little bit at a time. It called for continuity, persistence. And so, promising himself that he would give it his full attention if there were any developments, he decided to concentrate on his work for the time being. He was the most experienced person in his section. Even the division chief depended on him completely.

And then, five months after the trail had gone cold on the hill in Yoyogi, there was a development.

It was August. Within his section, people were planning their summer holidays. Asai thought he'd ask for the last week in September. He didn't like to take his leave during the hottest weather. He had no interest in going to the mountains or the sea. He'd never been much into sports, and he didn't have any kids to pester him to take them.

Asai had been deliberately vague about the time he wanted off, and had no specific plans. There was nowhere he really wanted to go. To tell the truth, he was busy at work and didn't really mind giving up his holidays. He'd always been like that; he enjoyed working. Relaxing was for the idle. Asai supposed that from an outsider's point of view he must have seemed like a very boring kind of husband.

One day towards the end of August, Asai was on the underground. He wasn't like the young people today, commuting by car. He hated the traffic – it made him irritable and wasted time. It was much cooler and quicker by train. He opened the weekly news publication that he'd just bought at the station. There was a special feature: *How many people would perish if a massive earthquake were to hit Tokyo?* That's right, thought Asai, five days from now it'll be 1 September – Disaster Prevention Day. Every year the newspapers and weeklies were full of these kinds of articles. Asai wasn't old enough to have experienced the Great Kanto Earthquake.

On 1 September 1923, the Great Kanto Earthquake hit. In Tokyo its magnitude was 7.9 on the Richter scale; 6 on the Japanese scale. It took the lives of 600,000 residents; in fact, far more died in the ensuing fires than were crushed to death in the quake itself. The current population of Tokyo is twelve million, about three times what it was in 1923. Tokyo today has a high concentration of high-rise buildings, and densely packed residential areas in which multi-unit apartment blocks proliferate. And it is forever expanding. If, for example, an earthquake of the exact same magnitude as 1923 were to strike present-day Tokyo, just how many victims would it claim? We took the predictions of several eminent authorities and prepared…

Because this was a disaster that could happen to anybody, the article was trying to stir up a mix of curiosity and unease in its readers. It also included lessons about what to do when the critical moment came.

Asai rested the back of his head against the train window and kept reading. He was dressed in a short-sleeved shirt and tie. He'd folded his jacket neatly and placed it on his lap. It was vital to have a jacket with you, even in the middle of summer, in case you had to meet an important client. And the tie was a mark of dignity among government officials at the ministry.

The article went on to say that if an earthquake the size of the Great Kanto one were to hit today, at least 560,000 people would be killed. According to different data, the number might reach one million. Of these, only around two thousand would be crushed by falling structures; the rest would die in fires, a repeat of the past.

In the worst possible scenario, the roads would become jammed with traffic, preventing people from escaping on foot. Because of huge crowds of people all trying simultaneously to escape, getting away by car would be an impossibility. There'd be jostling between pedestrians and drivers. Fights would break out. Everything would be overcome by fire and smoke, and there'd be nowhere left to run. Human beings would be burned alive.

Cars would catch fire, too. All along the streets, vehicles would start exploding. It would be as if petrol tanks had been lined up along all the streets of Tokyo. And the petrol stations as well. Every five hundred yards or so throughout the city each petrol station would ignite, adding to the fires. It was possible that more people would die from these fires than from being trapped inside a burning building. This was something that hadn't happened in 1923.

Throughout the city there were designated evacuation points, in parks, schools and the grounds of shrines or temples, but they wouldn't be able to accommodate the flood of people. Many would be burned before they even got there. The only thing this kind of evacuation plan was good for was to reassure people that there were measures in place. The underground gas lines that crisscrossed the city would be exposed by cracks in the ground and shoot flames into the air.

This is not a fairy tale. There is a real chance that this kind of extreme disaster could occur. Almost half a century has passed since the Great Kanto Earthquake. Everyone lives in fear of what might happen. This year alone, there have already been twenty-three earthquakes that could be detected by humans. Eleven of these measured 2 on the Japanese scale, and three measured 3. Of these, the level 3 earthquake that hit on 7 March at 3.25 in the afternoon caused many objects to fall off shelves. A significant number of people ran out into the street. Even though top experts claim that this is not a sign that the big one is imminent, the citizens of Tokyo cannot be reassured by words alone. There is no such thing as an absolute guarantee.

Asai went about his working day as usual. But that morning, something was bothering him and affecting his ability to concentrate: the newspaper article predicting the massive earthquake in Tokyo. Well, not the whole thing.

It had been just one short phrase buried in the middle of the scaremongering article that had disturbed him: "... *the level 3 earthquake that hit Tokyo on 7 March at 3.25 in the afternoon...*"

He'd been in Kobe on 7 March, so he hadn't been aware there had been an earthquake in Tokyo. Doctor Ohama had estimated his wife's time of death at around 4.05 p.m. that day. Was there some link between the earthquake and Eiko's death?

Asai pondered this possible connection. He wouldn't have said that Eiko was particularly afraid of earthquakes. If you lived in Tokyo, you got used to them. Even with the heart trouble that she had, the shock of a tremor probably wasn't enough to trigger a heart attack. He couldn't recall her ever panicking before when an earthquake had hit.

Asai went downstairs to get lunch at the staff canteen. As he ate his curry and rice, he decided to ask a question of the young man sitting across from him, sipping a glass of cream soda.

"Have you read that article in the latest edition of *R-Weekly* predicting a huge earthquake in the Tokyo area?"

"No, I haven't seen that one." The other man pulled a face, as if to say he had no interest in anything other than the immediate present.

"Well, in the article it said that there was a strong earthquake on the seventh of March in Tokyo. Do you remember?"

"The seventh of March?" The man raised his eyes to the ceiling, apparently in an effort to recollect the date.

"I was on a business trip to Kansai, so I wasn't here at the time, but according to the article it was a level 3 – strong enough for things to fall off shelves. It said quite a number of people ran out into the streets. Level 3 is pretty strong."

"Now you mention it, there was an earthquake," replied the young man. "I couldn't tell you the exact date, but there was one around the beginning of spring. This building was fine, but my wife said that a few things fell off the shelves at home. She said that our neighbour's grandfather clock stopped."

"Was your wife frightened?"

"She said it wasn't particularly scary. The house creaked and groaned a bit, but it soon stopped. It was cold, so she didn't bother going outside."

In Tokyo, for earthquakes to be a lively topic of conversation they had to be fairly significant. People were never particularly surprised by a couple of lightweight items falling from shelves.

Asai went back up to his division and entered the reference room. He borrowed a pocket digest of March newspaper articles, and turned to the 8 March morning editions. There was a very small feature on the earthquake towards the end.

At 3.25 p.m. on 7 March, there was a strong level 3 earthquake in the Tokyo area. Local residents were startled by items falling from shelves. According to the meteorological office, the earthquake was centred off the Boso Peninsula, at a depth of fifty kilometres below sea level.

Well, not all residents had been startled; that was embellishment on the journalist's part. Asai flicked through some of the previous pages and came across a weather map.

From the evening of the 6th and lasting all day of the 7th, a cold front will pass through the Kanto area. Temperatures will be around three degrees cooler than average. There is a possibility of snow in mountainous areas.

Asai left the reference room.

"It was cold, so she didn't bother going outside." This was what the junior colleague had said. It had been warm in Kansai. By the time Asai had arrived back in Tokyo the next morning, the cold front had already passed on, and he didn't recall it being particularly chilly.

Still, he couldn't connect the 7 March earthquake with Eiko's heart attack, and the presence of a cold front even less. He decided to banish the magazine article to the back of his mind.

On 1 September there was no earthquake.

One Sunday in the middle of September, a member of Eiko's haiku circle turned up to deliver a copy of the Haiku Association's newsletter. Mieko Suzuki was the woman who had encouraged Eiko to join – one of her old school friends.

Written on the cover page of the newsletter was the title "Eiko Asai Memorial Collection".

After paying her respects at the family's Buddhist altar, Ms Suzuki explained about the special collection.

"Our teacher selected around fifty poems out of the hundred and fifty or so that Eiko had composed," she explained.

"Eiko wrote a hundred and fifty haiku?"

Asai's lack of interest in haiku meant that he'd never paid any attention to the poems his wife had written. He'd felt the same way about the singing and the painting lessons, and hadn't realized that his wife had been such a prolific writer.

"It was a case of quantity over quality, I imagine," he said.

"No. Absolutely not. They were true works of art. If only she'd lived longer, she'd have ended up with a body of work that none of us could have held a candle to. Our teacher was truly devastated by her death. It's not flattery – it's the truth."

"I'm sure Eiko would have been happy to hear that."

Asai began to flick through the magazine. The memorial collection appeared right at the beginning, arranged by date of composition, and spanned the last two years.

Asai stopped at two of the most recent poems: *"Solemn Somin Shorai and the spring cow"* and *"The blossoming light of the golden Yamaga lantern"*. He looked puzzled.

"What do these two titles mean?"

"Somin Shorai is the name of a god who protects against evil. The haiku was written about a kind of amulet that you can get from a temple. This one is a little hexagonal tower, carved out of wood and bearing Somin Shorai's name. Apparently it's hand-painted and very delicate. Depending on the region it comes from, the shapes, sizes and designs of these amulets are different. But they all have a solemn or majestic quality."

"Is it a religious artefact?"

"More like a kind of talisman."

"What about the spring cow?"

"There was a cow in the temple grounds where she got the talisman. The contrast between the solemn talisman and the laid-back cow in the springtime was amusing."

"Is there a temple like that in or around Tokyo?"

Eiko had taken part in tours that visited famous spots, seeking inspiration for her poetry. She'd often wandered around by herself too.

"Hmm. I'm not sure. I've never heard of a place like that, but it might not be real. It might be a landscape that she imagined in her poem."

"And what's the Yamaga lantern in this other poem?"

"Yamaga is a hot-spring resort in Kumamoto Prefecture. Since olden days they've had a custom of making lanterns out of paper and offering them at the local shrine. But these are not just any old lanterns – they're elaborate palaces and castles, sometimes theatre sets, all made completely out of paper. She wrote 'golden', so that particular lantern must have been constructed from gold-leaf paper. I may have heard her mention it was a souvenir from a trip to Yamaga. I believe that's what she told the teacher when she submitted the poem."

"I don't think Eiko ever visited the Kyushu area."

"Then she must have seen it somewhere else. Perhaps she went to a department store when they had a special exhibit of products from Kyushu or something. She saw the gold-coloured lantern with the flower pattern and it gave her the idea of the blossoming light. This particular haiku is rather vivid and elegant. Also perfectly feminine. Eiko always had a very rich imagination. I admit I was a little envious."

"Really?" From singing to painting, then on to haiku – she'd had a very creative side, after all.

"She was such a lovely person, taken from us too soon. I can't imagine how you must feel." Ms Suzuki spoke as if she was amazed that Asai could manage alone with no one but the solitary elderly woman from the neighbourhood who came to help out in the daytime.

At the end of September there was a personnel reshuffle. A new division chief was brought in, and Asai became assistant division chief. A promotion for a non-career-track civil servant like him was awarded on merit. If he could just hang in there, the next step was division chief.

In the end, Asai never took his summer vacation days.

The new division chief invited Asai to his home in Harajuku for dinner. At the end of the evening, Asai set off for home in the car his boss had ordered for him, but on the way he suddenly changed his mind; Yoyogi wasn't far at all from Harajuku. It had been a while since he'd visited the hill where his wife had died, and it wouldn't take too long by car.

The driver turned around. They arrived at the top of the hill by a different route from the one Asai was used to. They passed by the Midori and came out by the entrance to the Tachibana. It was after 9 p.m. and the neon sign flickered in the night sky. It had been six months since he'd last seen this view.

"You want me to take this road downhill?" asked the driver, glancing back at him.

"Yes, please."

Asai, watching the view ahead through the front windscreen, suddenly lost track of where he was. The road looked different from this angle. There was a tall building ahead to the left, with a neon sign on the roof: HOTEL CHIYO.

The red of the neon stood out, vivid against the dark background of private homes. It was brand new. Even from this viewpoint, the sign dominated the skyline. There had been nothing like it here before. Asai had lost his bearings.

As the car continued down the hill, he peered out of the left side window. The building was a brand-new, three-storey hotel, with a very wide facade; Takahashi Cosmetics had disappeared. But the taxi passed by too fast, and in a flash the view was gone.

"Just a minute!" Asai hurriedly got the driver to stop. "This is fine. I'll get out here. I just remembered something I need to do."

The driver walked around and opened the car door.

"Should I wait for you?"

"No, no. It's fine. I'm going to be a while. Please go ahead and leave."

Asai turned and started to walk back up the hill.

9

Asai stood opposite the new three-storey hotel, by the house with the bamboo trees and the concrete wall. When he'd first visited Takahashi Cosmetics with his sister-in-law, he'd noted that the house had belonged to someone named Kobayashi. Now, the carved stone nameplate was tinged faintly red by the neon across the road.

The hotel was built in the latest fashionable style. Part Southern European, part replica of ancient European architecture, it was elegant, but nothing could hide the fact that it was a couples' hotel.

And it had just sprung up out of nowhere. It had been only six months since Asai had last been in the area. Somewhere within that short time frame, Takahashi Cosmetics and the next-door house with the bamboo fence and the zelkova tree had been torn down, the ground reworked, and architects and construction companies had moved in to put up this new building. Asai hadn't witnessed any of that. Right now, all he could do was stand and stare in amazement.

The name Chiyo obviously came from Chiyoko Takahashi's given name. The little cosmetics boutique, now vanished off the face of the earth, must once have stood right at the far end of what were now the hotel's white perimeter walls. Within those walls was a line of European-style cypresses, interspersed with what were probably intended to resemble European chestnut trees but were more likely Japanese horse chestnuts. They were planted close together to give some sort of wooded ambiance. And the tallest tree in the neighbourhood, the big old zelkova, was nowhere to be seen.

The low stone wall, the bamboo fence lined by azalea bushes: these were all gone and replaced with white concrete. There was a gently sloping terrace where a lawn had been planted, and a broad, sweeping driveway along which cars could enter the grounds. It looked like the entrance to a park.

What on earth had happened to the original house with its roofed gateway and stone steps? The two-storey house visible behind the trees and shrubs had been a typical old Japanese-style house. That property alone had had over a hundred yards of bamboo fence facing the street. When put together with the plot on which Takahashi Cosmetics had stood, it meant this hotel was built on a very generous portion of land indeed.

The original house had belonged to someone named Kubo, Asai recalled. When he'd visited with Miyako, he'd been paying attention to the surroundings, and had made a point of reading nameplates. Asai guessed that the Kubo family had bought up the neighbouring property in order to construct a hotel. But if that was the case, why the striking similarity of the hotel's name to Chiyoko Takahashi's? Perhaps the characters weren't supposed to read "Chiyo" at all, but "Sendai", meaning "one thousand generations", and it was just a coincidence. He couldn't imagine how the unmarried female proprietor, who couldn't even afford to hire staff to run her tiny cosmetics boutique, would have had the means to buy up the neighbouring plot of land and build a fancy hotel.

Or maybe someone else had purchased both the Kubo house and Takahashi Cosmetics. After all, the couples' hotel business was extremely profitable. It was a quiet area, and an exclusive neighbourhood to boot. The clientele would enjoy the high-end feel of the place, and after dark there were few passers-by to observe the couples coming and going. The street was poorly lit, too; infinitely preferable to a bustling, brightly lit street in the city centre. It seemed that up at the top of the hill, the Tachibana and Midori were both doing brisk business. Anyone with enough capital would recognize this area as a good investment opportunity.

According to the president of Yagishita Ham, back when he had visited Asai at the ministry, a lot of these kinds of hotel were popping up in hot-spring resorts. The regular Japanese inns were suffering from a shortage of maids and other attendants, and customer service was falling short. Compared to the traditional Japanese inn experience, a visit to a couples' hotel required far fewer personnel, and the room turnover rate was much higher. The facilities themselves were generally all that were required to turn a profit. Of course, the top-end villas and inns remained as they were, but the less popular hotels were rushing to convert.

Yet Asai couldn't help feel that something was oddly amiss. He was standing at the exact point on the road that his wife had been walking before her death from a sudden heart attack. If the maid at the Midori's account could be trusted, a brand-new couples' hotel had now suddenly appeared at the exact same location. It was a strange coincidence: the boutique where Eiko had taken her last breath had now become part of that same hotel.

After arriving at the ministry the next morning, Asai asked one of his junior colleagues to get him a copy of any documents relating to the ownership of the Hotel Chiyo from the Yoyogi local public office. When he opened the papers, his eyes widened; Chiyoko Takahashi was indeed listed as president. Well, he had half expected it, but it was still a surprise. How was that possible? Takahashi Cosmetics hadn't exactly been doing a roaring trade. He'd only been inside the boutique once, but after that, every time he'd passed by, the place had been empty. He'd never seen a single customer in there. There was no call for any extra staff – even the proprietor herself had nothing much to do.

When he'd visited to offer his thanks, Ms Takahashi had admitted she hadn't much business at the boutique. She dealt only in high-end cosmetic brands for her well-heeled clientele, but had confessed that she hadn't picked the right moment to invest. In other words, she had let it slip that her business was failing. She was an attractive woman, and Asai had been affected by her enough to feel sorry for the poor state of her business.

Yet it now turned out that this woman had had the funds to build a hotel. The money clearly hadn't come from the boutique.

Asai examined the list of executives on the document. Among them was someone called Konosuke Kubo. He was listed as a board member. Kubo? Oh yes, Kubo. That had been the name on the gate of the house next door.

You never knew when it came to money. People could appear to be operating in the depths of poverty, but have hidden assets elsewhere. Flourishing businesses might secretly be on the brink of bankruptcy. Sometimes a financial saviour might appear out of nowhere to save the day.

What about Chiyoko Takahashi? She appeared to be single, but she might well be looked after by a hidden patron, some kind of sugar daddy. Miyako had already pointed out that there was something a little flirtatious about her. And if a woman thought it too, then Asai guessed he was probably on the right track. He recalled that waft of perfume when she'd helped him on with his coat.

Her inventory was all expensive, brand-name goods, many of them imported. Even though the boutique was tiny, that would all have required a fair amount of capital. Yes, she must have had a patron to help finance the business. Even if she'd been single all her life, at some point she must have caught the eye of a man.

It was quite a change from cosmetics shop owner to director of a couples' hotel. But when he thought about it, he could understand why. She'd opened her high-end boutique in that neighbourhood with the hope of catering to the local residents. Assuming that she had a nose for business and her environment, she would have quickly understood the appeal of those hotels up the hill. Somehow, she'd found a way to persuade her neighbour,

Mr Kubo, to part with his house. She must have paid through the nose for it, though.

The name Konosuke Kubo appeared on the list of company board members. If this was her next-door neighbour, then he must have played a part in the hotel's construction; for instance, by providing his own land for the location. It was fairly common practice.

However, if Mr Kubo had been so instrumental in the process, then why didn't he hold a higher position in the company? He wasn't listed as managing director. The post of executive director was taken by a Sachiko Takahashi, possibly Chiyoko's sister. Provision of the land for a project was a substantial investment. Surely he should be the one listed as president, or, at the very least, some kind of director? Why had he been relegated to the lowly role of board member?

Asai's train of thought was broken by the arrival of the department director. Three visitors were waiting for him. They presented Asai with their name cards, showing they all belonged to the Yamagata Prefectural Agricultural Cooperative. The director made the introductions.

"As part of the integrated agricultural initiative, this agricultural cooperative is planning to establish several new food-processing plants. Specifically, ham and sausage factories. Up until now they've been in the canned-fruit business, but they're planning to expand into the meat industry. Accordingly, they have come to ask for advice on both the technology and distribution of these products. Asai, I'd like you to give them a general overview."

The leader of the cooperative dropped the name of a politician – "Mr So-and-So has been very encouraging", or something like that – but it was clear that he was letting the civil servants know that he had the power of an elected official behind him.

Asai, in his role as assistant division chief, began to talk them through it. Food processing was his field of expertise. He'd visited many, many factories and had become an authority on the subject. For the most part, his knowledge had been acquired through his work with Yagishita Ham.

Even as he was speaking, though, Asai's mind wandered back to the Hotel Chiyo.

How on earth could Konosuke Kubo be satisfied with his position as a regular board member? Perhaps he was simply the quiet, self-effacing type when it came to business matters. On the other hand, was he purposely trying to hide his connection but secretly had a great deal of power and influence? Either could be possible.

What was the relationship between Chiyoko Takahashi and Konosuke Kubo? Were they no more than neighbours? Or were they neighbours who saw an opportunity to make money and became business partners? Or was it something else?

Asai realized he'd come to the end of his spiel when the voice of one of his visitors broke into his thoughts.

"We'd like to observe a meat-processing plant – ham and sausages, if possible. Could you suggest somewhere we could go?"

Asai had been thinking about the new hotel the whole time he'd been speaking. In fact, he was so familiar with the ins and outs of administrative guidance that he could have made the whole speech in his sleep.

"I'd recommend the Yagishita Ham Corporation in Kobe. They're very experienced in the field and equipped with state-of-the-art machinery. They've recently opened their second branch, here in Higashi Murayama."

Of course, he didn't mention his special relationship with Mr Yagishita.

"This is the current size of our pig-farming operations. How much would we need to expand?"

Asai listened to the details of their current operation and replied with the appropriate figure.

The director then decided to slip in a few words of flattery. "We are aware that most local farming communities are currently experiencing rather a negative response to the recent government policy regarding diversion of farmland, so I respect your forward-thinking approach."

"Forward-thinking approach" was the kind of empty phrase beloved of politicians. The director loved to use it every time agricultural cooperative officials paid the ministry a visit.

Unimpressed by his boss's choice of words, Asai let his mind wander once again.

What if Konosuke Kubo was Chiyoko Takahashi's secret patron? They lived right next door to one another so it was definitely possible. If that was the case, then they must have built the hotel together, Kubo deliberately keeping a low profile as far as the paper trail was concerned. The man lived in that huge mansion. Asai had no idea what his line of work might be, but there was no doubt that he was wealthy.

But, then, what a brazen act for Ms Takahashi to have a boutique next to Mr Kubo's home. What man would be so shameless as to set his mistress up in business right next door? Perhaps he'd got it all wrong after all…

He was suddenly jolted out of his reverie.

"Would it be at all possible in the near future for you to pay a visit to our neck of the woods?"

Asai realized the chairman of the cooperative was addressing him.

"Pardon?"

"We would very much like you to visit our prefecture, Mr Asai. We're all pretty much novices in the field, so we'd appreciate any kind of guidance you can offer us."

The director turned to face Asai.

"I think you can probably make the time, can't you?"

It appeared the director was anxious to lend his support to the politician named by the men from Yamagata.

By the time Asai got back from his business trip, the background check he had ordered on Chiyoko Takahashi and Konosuke Kubo was finished and the report ready for him to pick up. A week before his departure, he had requested the help of a detective agency.

Out of a sense of self-preservation, Asai had decided not to reveal himself to be an assistant division chief at the Ministry of Agriculture and Forestry. He had visited the detective agency under a false name, explained what he needed to be investigated, and paid the necessary deposit. He gave a made-up address and told them he didn't have a phone line. He arranged to call them to find out when the report was ready and go to pick it up in person, at which time he would pay the balance of the fee.

He called the agency the day of his return from Yamagata, and was told that the investigation was complete. He took a taxi over right away, kept his promise to pay the balance, and left with a large envelope. This way, he believed, no one would have an inkling who it was who had requested the investigation into Ms Takahashi and Mr Kubo.

The report read as follows:

Chiyoko Takahashi, 36 years old, married Fumitaro Ozawa, a trader from Yokohama, twelve years ago. They were divorced five years ago. The reason for the divorce was her husband's extramarital affair. She received a very generous amount of money as a settlement, but the exact amount cannot be verified. Mr Ozawa immediately remarried.

Following her divorce, Chiyoko Takahashi managed a hair salon in Shinagawa, but having no formal training, she didn't cut her customers' hair herself. She seemed to have a talent for management, however, and the salon was popular. Around that time she had an affair with the owner of a wholesale cosmetics business. There was trouble when the trader's wife found out. From time to time she'd turn up at Ms Takahashi's shop, which caused a scandal. It became uncomfortable for Ms Takahashi to stay in the neighbourhood, so three years ago she moved to Sanya in Yoyogi and opened a small shop selling cosmetics. The wholesaler's name is Genkichi Higai, aged 52. He has a store in Kyobashi, and is rather wealthy. It was with Mr Higai's assistance that Ms Takahashi opened her Yoyogi boutique, and it appears that they are still lovers. This year, she bought a ten-thousand-square-foot plot of land from her next-door neighbour, Konosuke Kubo. She combined this land with the thousand square feet she already had, and built the Hotel Chiyo. It can be assumed that most of the funds for the purchase were provided by Genkichi Higai. The aforementioned Konosuke Kubo is listed as a board member of the corporation, and Ms Takahashi has let slip that he demanded a percentage of the profits of the new hotel in return for agreeing to sell his land. It was supposedly Higai who conducted the negotiations. The hotel is doing very well.

Of course; it was just as he'd guessed. Chiyoko Takahashi was no lonely divorcee. She may not have been a stunning beauty, but she was an attractive, mature woman. He hadn't believed she was completely single, and, sure enough, she'd turned out to have a patron. A hair salon and a cosmetics shop that needed stock; wholesale cosmetics – it all made sense. A relationship that had started out with the provision of goods had turned into a love affair.

The shop that, despite its tiny size, had such a vast and expensive inventory; the purchase of the neighbouring land; the construction of an attractive, European-style hotel – the detective's report made perfect sense.

Konosuke Kubo, 38 years old. Married for ten years to Kazuko (aged 32), no children. The house in Yoyogi was built about fifty years ago by his father, who was a wholesaler of silk goods. Konosuke was born in that house, and lived there up until its sale to the hotel corporation.

Konosuke Kubo graduated from the commerce department at a certain private university, and following his father's death took over the family business. The market went through a depression, and the company went under. Since then, he has been employed as the General Affairs manager at his uncle's textile firm, and lives the typical salaryman's lifestyle. With the failure of the family business, his fortune is not as great as it once was, but he has inherited land in several parts of the city. His reputation at work is reasonably good, and there have been no complaints regarding his conduct. Drinks moderately. Since the sale of his Yoyogi house, he has rented a single-roomed apartment on the third floor of the Keyaki Mansion building in Higashi Nakano.

His wife, Kazuko, has tuberculosis, and has been a patient at a sanatorium in the mountains of Nagano Prefecture for the past year and a half. Mr Kubo goes up to Nagano the last weekend of every month to visit. There are no rumours of any marital infidelities on his part.

Asai's theory – that there had been a sexual relationship between Chiyoko Takahashi and Konosuke Kubo – had been completely demolished by this report.

10

The detective agency's report had said that there was no personal relationship between Ms Takahashi and Mr Kubo, but Asai still had his doubts. Kubo didn't have any financial problems. He owned plots of land inherited from his father at various locations throughout Tokyo. The report didn't specify where exactly, but as the plots had been purchased by his father many years ago they must have been in the old city, or at least close to it. And close to it would mean in one of the newly developed sub-centres; either way, they must be worth a fortune. And he must receive a generous salary at his uncle's company. His father's business may have gone under with him at the helm, but that would have made little difference in the long run. He was still very well off indeed. And he only had his wife and himself to support.

Why would a man who wasn't short of money sell his family home to Chiyoko Takahashi and then move to a tiny apartment in Higashi Nakano? There was no doubt that his Yoyogi house would have been much more comfortable, and in a far pleasanter neighbourhood. At least it *had* been an upmarket, tasteful neighbourhood until all the hotels had invaded their peace. By law, local residents were permitted to block the construction of such places if they were within a school zone, but neighbourhoods outside school zones were powerless to do anything. Sometimes locals would join together and protest against construction projects, but it was always pretty much a lost cause. It was highly likely that the Yoyogi residents would have launched a protest against the building of the Chiyo right there on their hill, complaining that it was a blemish on their surroundings. He didn't need the money, so what had made Mr Kubo sell his land to a business venture that he should have abhorred and that he knew would scandalize the neighbourhood? And then become one of the executives of that same hotel?

Asai was sure there was more to the story. The agency's investigation had barely scratched the surface. A man not yet forty who'd sent his wife away to a distant sanatorium. A woman in her thirties, divorced and involved with the president of a medium-sized business. Put these two people next door to one another, and something could quite possibly come of it. Chiyoko Takahashi, although not traditionally beautiful, was certainly a charming woman. Well spoken and polite, skilfully applied make-up, a glimpse of flirtatiousness in her movements... It would be so easy for a man whose wife was hospitalized far away to lose his head over Ms Takahashi. He had surrendered his land to her and put his name behind an immoral business enterprise. What was really going on?

But it wasn't simply curiosity that kept Asai ruminating on all this; he knew that his wife had been taken ill right where Mr Kubo's house used to stand. And he had the strangest sense that Eiko herself might be the connection between Konosuke Kubo and Chiyoko Takahashi. The thought kept nagging at him that around the time of Eiko's death there had been a fairly strong earthquake, but he still didn't know if there was any connection between this earthquake and her death.

Ms Takahashi hadn't mentioned the earthquake, so it had probably happened before Eiko had run into her boutique. If that was the case, then she had no reason to bring it up. If, for instance, the tremor had hit while Eiko was lying down in the back of the shop, then it would surely have stuck in Ms Takahashi's memory, and she would have said something about it. Or was it because the inhabitants of Tokyo are so used to earthquakes that it hadn't even left an impression on her? Asai found he couldn't erase these thoughts from his head.

The other thing bothering him was Eiko's haiku. In her memorial collection there had been the poems about a Somin Shorai amulet, and a Yamaga lantern. Asai had never once heard his wife talk of these things. He was fairly sure she hadn't been into folk art or crafts. There was nothing like that in their home, and he'd never heard her mention buying anything at a department store. They must have been something she'd gone to see in an exhibition somewhere. He couldn't work out what on earth these objects and the haiku could have had to do with her sudden death, but they wouldn't stop playing on his mind.

Asai was dying to call at the Chiyo and take a look around, but he couldn't risk running into Chiyoko Takahashi. It wasn't just that he had no reason to be there, but if she really had been involved in Eiko's death in some way, he didn't want to alert her to his suspicions.

He was sure if he could just get into the hotel and look around there would be some sort of clue. Obviously there wouldn't be anything in full view, but he just might be able to discover something that would give him a hint as to the truth. He clung to this unlikely hope – well, maybe more of a fantasy – while at the same time his suspicions about Ms Takahashi and Mr Kubo kept growing.

He wouldn't get away with turning up at the hotel alone as he'd done the other times. The story about the abandoned husband searching for his estranged wife was not going to work. What if Chiyoko Takahashi appeared when he was in the middle of questioning one of the maids?

If he was going to check out the Hotel Chiyo, then he needed to find a woman to go with him. But he didn't know anyone. This wasn't an easy favour – he didn't know any women who would risk being seen going into a couples' hotel.

He had thought of his sister-in-law. She'd probably be sympathetic if he explained he was trying to find out the truth about her older sister's death, but Miyako was a married woman. Perhaps she'd be okay with it if he told her there was some definite proof on the other side of those walls, but the vague idea that he should go and take a look around wasn't going to convince her. And if he wasn't careful about how he brought it up, she might think he had another motive for inviting her to that sort of hotel. Well, no, he hoped she knew him better than that, but even so, what would they do when they got there? Putting on disguises and visiting the hotel would take some guts. And getting permission from her husband to do something like that? Not an option. The two of them going there on the quiet? Could lead to a fatal misunderstanding.

No, Asai was going to have to abandon his plan to pay a visit to the Chiyo until he could find himself a suitable companion.

Asai knew very well what Chiyoko Takahashi looked like, but he had never met Konosuke Kubo. What kind of man was he? What did he look like? He was curious to set eyes on him, just one time.

The detective agency had included Mr Kubo's address in Higashi Nakano in the report, right down to the apartment number. He also knew the address and telephone number of his workplace, R-Textiles in Kyobashi. Which would be the better location to get a look at Kubo without being seen?

He could loiter in the hallway in front of Kubo's apartment and watch for him going in or out, but there was no way to predict when he might appear, and if he hung around for too long the other residents or the apartment manager would get suspicious. It'd be like the time he'd been peering through the front window of Takahashi Cosmetics and probably been mistaken for a thief by the tall man standing behind him with his dog. If he hung around an apartment building, he was bound to be asked what he was doing there.

The other possibility was to visit R-Textiles. Unless he was out on business, Kubo should be easy to spot at his workplace, sitting in the General Affairs manager's office. Asai only needed to observe him from a distance. It would be the same as at Asai's own office – the corridors were always filled with anonymous visitors. It was just like any city street. Asai decided on this option.

Just after one in the afternoon, he let the division chief know he was going out, and set off walking towards the underground at Toranomon. From there, it was only twenty minutes to Kyobashi, and R-Textiles was less than a ten-minute walk from the station.

The company occupied about five rooms on the fourth floor of a tall office building. Asai couldn't make anything out beyond the panes of frosted glass that divided the rooms from the corridor. There was a nameplate on each door indicating the name of the company, but, unlike the ministry, there was nothing to say which section, so Asai couldn't guess which one housed the General Affairs division.

Asai was wearing dark glasses, in the hope that no one would get a good look at his face. Tinted glasses were popular these days, so no one would think it was strange. He'd worn them when he visited the detective agency too.

Asai hung around in the corridor, trying to look as if he were waiting for someone. Behind his glasses it was dark. Just as he was hoping a secretary or someone would come by, the door of the room closest to the lift opened and a young woman in a light-blue smock and miniskirt came out carrying a pile of documents. Asai went up to her.

"Excuse me, do you work for R-Textiles?"

"Yes," she said, looking up at him.

"Which room is the General Affairs section?"

"General Affairs? It's this one."

She pointed to the door she had just come through.

"Oh, I see. Er… is the manager, Mr Kubo, in the office right now?" He emphasized Kubo's name to make sure he had the right place.

"Yes, I think he's in."

"The General Affairs manager is Mr Konosuke Kubo, right?"

"Yes, that's right."

The young woman glanced once more at Asai's dark glasses.

"You see, I'm due at a meeting in one of the other offices in this building, but afterwards I have a meeting with Mr Kubo. Unfortunately it's the first time we'll have met face to face, so I thought I'd just come over first to check out what he looks like. Then I'll be able to walk straight up to him when I come to meet him later."

This wasn't the most plausible of excuses, but the woman didn't seem to care.

"Follow me, please," she said, opening the office door.

"Thank you."

Asai spoke softly. He took one step inside the door, right behind the young woman. He was a little nervous, expecting all the employees in the office to turn and stare at him, but he needn't have worried. It was a large office, chock-a-block with desks and overflowing with people, both standing and sitting. No one paid Asai any attention. The receptionist's desk, nearest to the doorway, was unoccupied.

"Which one is Mr Kubo?" he whispered to his guide.

"The general manager is over there."

She raised the pile of documents slightly so that she could discreetly point a finger. In the direction she indicated, towards the window, there were three large tables lined up together, around which five or six men were sitting or standing. Keeping his eyes on the men, Asai whispered once again to the young woman.

"Which one is he?"

"He's sitting at the far end of those three desks. The tall man. Wearing glasses. Look, he's talking to the deputy manager – the man standing across from him. That's Mr Kubo."

The woman glanced at Asai to check he was looking in the right direction.

"That man with glasses? The one who just put a cigarette in his mouth?"

Asai's throat seemed to have closed up.

"That's right. That's him."

"The one just lighting his cigarette now?"

"Yes."

Asai hurriedly thanked the young woman and got out of the room as fast as he could.

Mr Kubo, General Affairs manager, was the same man he'd seen last spring when he'd been trying to look inside Takahashi Cosmetics. The one standing behind him on the street, staring at him, dressed in a grey sweater and with a German shepherd. The same long face that had watched him beat a hasty retreat.

Asai made his way straight over to the detective agency in Kanda, where he was met by the same detective as before.

"I'd like to request a further investigation, please," he said, his dark glasses still firmly in place.

The man frowned.

"Oh, was there a problem with the first one?"

"No. Not at all. This time, I'd like you to focus the investigation on Konosuke Kubo."

"I see. What kind of things do you want to know?"

"His daily routine back when he lived in Yoyogi."

"His daily routine? Not now, but when he lived in the house in Yoyogi?"

"Well, I'm interested in his current lifestyle too, but for now just when he was in Yoyogi. Before his land was turned into a hotel."

"It was back at the end of April that his house was knocked down to make room for the hotel. It's going to be very difficult to find out much about his life before that, you know."

"I'm willing to pay whatever it takes."

"And you know, people aren't very community-spirited around that neighbourhood. They don't have much to do with one another. We're not going to get much out of interviewing his ex-neighbours. I'm not sure what the best approach would be." The detective folded his arms.

"I'm counting on you to find a way."

"All right. 'His daily routine' is a little vague. What specifically do you want to know?"

"First of all, whether he was home on the afternoon of the seventh of March."

The detective made a note.

"There was a strong earthquake at 3.25 that afternoon," Asai continued.

"An earthquake? What has that got to do with Kubo?"

"Maybe nothing. But that day there was a big earthquake, and you might be able to use the fact to jog people's memories."

"Got it. So you want me to find out whether Kubo was home at the time of the earthquake and what he was doing?"

"Yes. But not just during the earthquake. What he was doing that afternoon, until around four."

"And is there anything in particular you're interested in about that afternoon? If you could let me know, it might help me find some leads."

"Yes, I'd like to know if anyone visited Mr Kubo at home at any point in the afternoon."

"Ah, you mean a woman?"

The detective probably assumed that Asai meant Chiyoko Takahashi.

"Not only Ms Takahashi. I mean, she may well have visited him that afternoon, but if there was someone else..."

"Someone else?"

"Yes. Man or woman – it doesn't matter. Anyone who visited that house on the afternoon of the seventh."

He was being deliberately vague. He had Eiko in mind, but he didn't dare put that into words, even discreetly. If the detective knew the identity of the probable visitor, he would know too much about Asai.

"I don't think anyone would know that besides the people in the house," said the detective, pulling a face. "His wife's in a sanatorium up in Nagano. There's only the housekeeper who'd be able to help."

"The housekeeper? Of course. But in your previous report you wrote that Mr Kubo didn't have one. Just a part-time help."

"She was sent by a dispatch service."

"So if you ask the dispatch service, they'll let you talk to her?"

"I think so. But these services don't always send the same person every time. I'll make it a priority to find the one who worked on the seventh of March."

"It'd be useful if you could talk to others who worked on different days, to get an idea of Mr Kubo's daily routine, but let's find out about the seventh of March first. Do you think you'll be able to find her?"

"If she's still working for the dispatch service, and out on another job, I'll go and find her there and interview her. If she's quit the service, it might take a little longer to find her."

"I'd appreciate that."

"Understood. Is there anything else you'd like to know about?"

Asai thought for a moment.

"As a matter of fact there is. What are Mr Kubo's hobbies?"

11

Had it really been Konosuke Kubo watching him that day? Ever since he'd caught a glimpse of the face of the General Affairs manager at R-Textiles, the memory kept playing in Asai's head.

It had been a bright afternoon in early spring, and he'd been completely focused on trying to see through the gap in the front door of Takahashi Cosmetics. He'd felt someone standing behind him. He hadn't heard footsteps or a voice, but there'd been some sort of invisible force like a wave breaking against his back, and in response he had turned around to see the figure of a man with a dog standing at the other side of the road. Asai could tell that the man had been watching him for some time.

Asai had been worried at the time that he might be taken for a burglar, so he had stepped away from the shop window very slowly and calmly – he hadn't run in case that would have made him look even more suspicious – and begun to walk away in the opposite direction. Still, until he'd managed to put a reasonable distance between himself and the tall figure, he'd been afraid that the man would challenge him and demand to know what he was doing. His feet had felt clumsy, the flesh on his back crawling.

He had only turned and glimpsed the man's long face, and thanks to the backlighting effect of the sun it had been dark like an underexposed photograph. He couldn't make out anything clearly besides a nose and a pair of spectacles. As time had passed, these had become the stranger's distinguishing features. And now, as those features from his memory began to merge with the face of the man who'd been seated at the desk in the General Affairs department of R-Textiles, it had all suddenly come together.

The man with the dog who'd been staring at him that day hadn't been a concerned resident. He hadn't been out there watching over the shop out of kindness or consideration for his next-door neighbour. He'd had the look of someone defending his own property. His stance, the feel of his glare: there had been something very severe about him.

It made sense. If the man had been Kubo, Asai could see why he might have given him that strange look. If he had an intimate relationship with Ms Takahashi next door, he wouldn't have been able to ignore another man checking out her premises while she was out. If, after watching a little longer, he'd decided that Asai was a burglar, he might have set his German shepherd on him. Or perhaps he'd been suspicious that this snooper had some kind of relationship with Chiyoko Takahashi. Whichever of these might have been the truth, his behaviour had definitely been out of the ordinary.

Whatever the case, Asai wanted to know the exact nature of the relationship between Konosuke Kubo and Chiyoko Takahashi. And so he had ended up at the private detective agency once again. Had Ms Takahashi made Kubo a member of Hotel Chiyo's board of directors in return for the sale of the land, or was it much more than that? He was anxious to know the truth.

Asai had the advantage that Mr Kubo had never seen his face clearly. In front of the cosmetics shop there had been only a split second before Asai had turned and walked away. He was sure that Kubo had never got a proper look at him. At R-Textiles too, Asai had stayed right in the corner near the entrance; Kubo had been in conversation with other staff members, and had never once looked up. It was typical of any office – insurance salesmen and other businesspeople would often stop by the reception desk. Staff were used to this, and didn't pay them any attention. Nobody had even glanced in Asai's direction. Besides, he'd been wearing dark glasses, so no one could have seen his face clearly.

Some day he was going to run into Konosuke Kubo. When that happened, it was vital that the man didn't recognize him. Above all, he didn't want to be identified as Tsuneo Asai, husband of Eiko Asai. He mustn't be traced back to the Ministry of Agriculture and risk a stain on his reputation as a ministry civil servant. Kubo was not to recognize his face, know his name, or have an idea where he worked. He should be nothing more to him than an anonymous figure he saw on the street. On the other hand, Asai would know everything there was to know about Konosuke Kubo.

For the next two weeks, as he anxiously waited for the detective agency to complete the second investigation, Asai was distracted and unable to concentrate. He was impatient to hear what the housekeeper from the dispatch service had to say about Kubo's private life and the events of 7 March. The detective had told him he couldn't be sure whether she still worked for the service, but Asai held out hope he'd be able to find her.

It was surprising that one lone maid from a cleaning service had been employed to clean such a large house, but these days it was getting more and more difficult to find a live-in housekeeper. Asai supposed that as there was only Kubo and his wife, and as she was currently hospitalized, there wasn't any call for full-time live-in help. Or maybe that was why he had sold the house off – because it had become so difficult to keep it running without a permanent housekeeper. He'd heard many times that when a couple were on their own without children, living in an apartment was often the more practical and comfortable option.

Asai had long believed that there was a connection between Kubo's sale of the fine old house in a great neighbourhood and his relationship with Chiyoko Takahashi. He hadn't quite given up on that theory, but ever since he'd heard about the maid he'd employed from the dispatch service, he was anxious to hear what other evidence she might have.

Anyway, he was certain that the next investigation would make everything clear. What insight was he going to get into Kubo's private life? Was there a connection between him and Ms Takahashi?

Or was he hoping to find out whether Eiko had somehow played a part in Kubo's life?

Going to the detective agency under a false name, going back in person to pick up the report, paying in cash – all these were to make sure that the detective had no idea of his true identity. So if it turned out that Eiko was mixed up in all this, then the detective would have no idea that she was related to Asai in any way. He wouldn't feel the need to hide any of the details from his client.

In those weeks before the second report was completed, Asai made an effort to throw himself into his work. He was sent to Ishikawa and Yamanashi on government business. Farmers in both prefectures were interested in moving away from the cultivation of rice and developing their meat-processing industry. Asai went on a week's tour, invited by local agricultural cooperatives to give lectures on the meat industry in their town or village. The Ministry of Agriculture and Forestry had been trying to deal with the national rice surplus by getting farmers to reduce the acreage devoted to the cultivation of rice, but they knew their measures were inefficient. Local farming families also knew that this policy was doing nothing to improve their prospects. In the current recession, the present system of food control was just not working, and the future looked grim. The farmers felt that the recent trend of leaving the countryside in the off season to find outside work was not what their job should be about. Lately, even the women were being forced to go to the cities to find jobs to supplement their falling income.

It was here that the agricultural cooperatives came in. They were encouraging farming families to give up their little domestic sidelines – work traditionally performed by the grandparents and wives of farming families, such as the raising of pigs. The plan was to get whole communities to work together in joint enterprises, a more modern farming model which they considered to be better equipped to face the future.

Whenever there was a general election, the top executive of the local agricultural cooperative was in charge of collecting votes from its members, and when the time came for the government to hold meetings to decide the latest price of rice, he was also the man responsible for lining up the protesters in front of the Ministry of Agriculture. Today, this same man was delivering the opening greetings for Asai's lecture.

Asai, while maintaining what he believed to be the dignity appropriate to a government employee, explained manufacturing techniques and business methods. He didn't limit his talks to meat products; he also covered fruit and, in the coastal areas, the processing of seafood and other marine products. For this he had an official from the Fisheries Agency accompanying him. For meat and fruit, Asai had enough general background knowledge of the industry to get the job done by himself. A veteran administrator in the field of food processing, he had a vast amount of technical knowledge, more even than some of the specialist technicians employed in the industry.

Asai was very well-received out in the provinces. The inns he stayed in were not luxurious, but the meals he was served were made from the freshest ingredients. Sometimes there were geishas attending the evening parties. His only problem on the trip was trying to keep up with the large number of heavy drinkers who wanted to toast his good health. And in the daytime he had a chance to visit some of the local tourist spots.

He was pretty much fully occupied with all this, but there were also free moments when his mind drifted back to the investigation. How much had they found out so far?

There were plenty of people envious of Asai's newly single status. Several of his colleagues at the ministry expressed their views.

"Must be nice to be free."

"You can come home as late as you like, even stay out all night, and no wife at home to complain. We're all kind of jealous of you."

"You can do whatever you want, enjoy a whole second youth. Unfortunately for me, my wife has me under her thumb."

However, Asai wasn't the type to play around. He had never cheated on his wife, or even thought about it. He knew everything there was to know about being a civil servant, but had never had the faintest idea how to attract women. He'd never had a passionate love affair. He knew all too well that he just didn't have that kind of appeal to the opposite sex. And consequently he had never even tried to pick up a woman. Even if he'd wanted to, he just didn't have the courage. His interest in women had long been on the back burner. And so, even though others were envious of his return to bachelorhood, for him it was no hedonistic freedom. Perhaps if he'd had more money, things would have been different, but he didn't have that luxury. He had no intention of dipping into his precious funds month after month to pay for prostitutes.

Some of his more outspoken colleagues asked him when he was going to get married again. They thought he might be able to get himself a young wife, and that also made them envious.

He'd not even thought about that yet. He supposed he might after the first anniversary of Eiko's death. There were people who loved to play matchmaker, but Asai really wasn't inclined to rush into something. A woman of his age would have a past. He didn't want to be compared to someone else, and didn't think another marriage like that would work out. A plain, quiet wife would be a problem. He wasn't at all outgoing or flamboyant, so between them it would be one gloomy, cheerless household. He'd much prefer a cheerful, intellectual, kind wife with feminine charms, but this was hardly likely for a forty-something civil servant on his third marriage. There were very few possibilities left; he knew his prospects were bleak. Asai was confident of his abilities and achievements as a civil servant, but it was a completely different matter when it came to his private life.

And anyway, he wouldn't know how to relate to a young wife. She was bound to cheat on him. He'd have no idea what she was up to outside the house. Eiko had caused him more than enough trouble with private detectives.

Finally, he was informed that the second investigation was complete. Asai donned his usual dark glasses and set out for the detective agency. He was met once again by the chief detective.

"We eventually managed to find the maid from the cleaning service. She'd left the company and was working for a different place. It took a lot of running around by one of our junior staff, but finally he found out she'd gone back to her hometown in rural Yamanashi Prefecture. That's why the fee ended up being a little higher than we anticipated."

"I'll pay the extra."

"I'm confident that we've put together a report that you'll find very satisfying. Here it is."

He produced a similar large envelope to last time, the flap sealed with tape. It looked every bit like important, classified information. The envelope looked bulkier than last time.

Asai ripped off the tape. Inside was traditional Japanese paper, printed with blue characters. CONFIDENTIAL had been stamped in red ink in the top right-hand corner of each sheet of paper.

Testimony of Komako Hanai, 35 years old. According to Ms Hanai, she was dispatched by a maid service to the home of Konosuke Kubo in Sanya, Yoyogi between October of last year and March of this year, to work as a part-time housekeeper. This was not a live-in post – she would arrive at the said address around 7.30 a.m., and return to the maid service living quarters around 7 p.m. Below is her detailed account of Mr Kubo's daily routine.

Asai read up to this point, then returned the paper to the envelope.

"I'll pay right now. How much do I owe you?"

After settling his account, Asai went to a nearby café to read the rest of the report.

Komako Hanai had three days off a month, but these days weren't specified in advance. They were made by arrangement between Ms Hanai and Mr Kubo. Her duties included preparing meals, cleaning, laundry, etc. According to Ms Hanai, as Mr Kubo lived alone, there wasn't too much laundry. As he used to send most of his clothes to a dry cleaner's, it was a very light load indeed. The toughest job was the cleaning. Both the house and garden were very big, and it would have been impossible to clean every corner. However, Mr Kubo gave instructions that she only need clean the areas he habitually used. She was only required to tidy up the part of the garden directly around the front entranceway. Mr Kubo looked after the German shepherd dog that he kept by the back door himself. He was fond of dogs, and told Ms Hanai that he used to have an Akita and a collie.

Mr Kubo ate a light, western-style breakfast and took lunch at his office (on his days off he also ate bread for lunch) and fish or meat for dinner, but he wasn't particular about his meals. If he was going to be late home from work, or had a work-related dinner, he would usually let Ms Hanai know in advance. If there was an unexpected change of plan, and he was coming home early, he would call her. On these occasions she was free to lock up and leave around four in the afternoon.

Mr Kubo's wife was in a sanatorium in Nagano Prefecture, so Ms Hanai barely ever went into her room to clean. It seemed Mr Kubo dealt with the cleaning of that part of the house himself. Ms Hanai guessed it was because there were some valuable items in her room. Anyway, Mr Kubo didn't want her in there.

With no children and a wife away in a sanatorium, Mr Kubo seemed to lead a rather lonely life. He wasn't the type to play around, and didn't seem to be having any affairs as far as Ms Hanai could tell. He didn't play golf or mah-jong; his hobbies were reading and collecting traditional handcrafted toys. He had a collection that included examples of the most important and famous artefacts from around the country. All the display shelves in his drawing room, his study, his living room were filled with these toys. He had a particularly large collection of paper kites, many of them on display on the walls of his drawing and living rooms. There were even some hanging from the ceiling. Mr Kubo was very fond of handmade paper toys, and among them was a particularly beautiful theatre stage and lantern made of delicate paper. When Ms Hanai asked him about them, he told her that they were Yamaga lanterns from Higo.

There was a blinding explosion of white light before Asai's eyes.

The blossoming light of the golden Yamaga lantern.

It was at Konosuke Kubo's house that Eiko had seen it.

He'd had a sense of foreboding up to now, but this very precise proof took his breath away. The café's low background music made a high-pitched assault on his ears and set his heart thumping. His eyes began to race rapidly across the remaining lines on the paper.

According to Komako Hanai, Mr Kubo and his neighbour, Chiyoko Takahashi, had practically no contact at all. She was no more to him than the owner of the cosmetics shop next door. If they met on the street they exchanged a greeting, but that was about it. In all the time that Ms Hanai worked for Mr Kubo, she had not once seen Ms Takahashi set foot inside the house. Nor had Mr Kubo ever gone next door to visit Ms Takahashi. Of course, this was only during the hours that Ms Hanai was at the Kubo house. It was possible that the two had met after seven in the evening when Ms Hanai had gone home. And she had no idea what happened on her days off. However, if the two did have an intimate relationship, she believed there would have been something in their behaviour, and she certainly hadn't noticed anything.

As previously mentioned, Ms Hanai had three days off a month. Each time, the two would agree on the date, but mostly Mr Kubo was the one to approach her two or three days in advance and indicate a date that suited him. He never seemed to choose a Sunday. She believed that Mr Kubo went to work on the days in question. In addition, Mr Kubo would always go to visit his wife on the last Saturday of the month, staying overnight in Nagano. This was also a day off for Ms Hanai.

The 7 March was a Friday. Mr Kubo had arranged with Ms Hanai two days in advance for her to have that day off. When she came in early the next morning, the house was not in its usual state.

One of the tatami mats in the living room had been burnt and left outside the back door. One of the *fusuma* paper sliding doors had also been burnt from floor level up to about halfway. There were three recently used buckets scattered around the kitchen floor. A lot of the other tatami flooring and door partitions were soaking wet. The gas heater in the living room was also wet. It clearly looked like the aftermath of a fire.

Ms Hanai was very surprised and asked Mr Kubo what had happened. Mr Kubo replied that while he had been in the toilet a lit cigarette had accidentally fallen onto his newspaper, which caught fire, spreading to the tatami and *fusuma*. He'd come back, and in a panic had fetched water from the kitchen and thrown it over the room to put out the fire. Luckily he'd caught it before it had turned into something serious. It seemed that on 7 March Mr Kubo had been at home all day.

12

Asai's wife hadn't died in Takahashi Cosmetics after all; she'd already been dead when she arrived. Or at least that was what Asai deduced from the report's contents. He was led to conclude that from the points below.

1. The maid, Komako Hanai, had not visited the Kubo house on 7 March, and Kubo had taken that day off work. It could be assumed that he spent the whole day at home.

2. When Ms Hanai arrived at the house on the morning of the eighth, she discovered that a section of the tatami flooring and one partition of the paper doors had been burnt. Kubo told her that his cigarette had set fire to a newspaper while he'd been in the toilet, but he'd put the fire out before it got too big. There was also evidence that water had been thrown over the gas heater.

3. There were three buckets in the kitchen which had presumably been used to put out the fire. None of the buckets was dry – they all had water in the bottom.

4. There was a level 3 earthquake in Tokyo at 3.25 p.m. on 7 March. The newspaper had characterized it as

strong enough to cause objects to fall off shelves, and wrote that "many people ran out into the street".

5. In another newspaper Asai had read the following: "From the evening of the 6th and lasting all day of the 7th, a cold front will pass through the Kanto area. Temperatures will be around three degrees cooler than average. There is a possibility of snow in mountainous areas."

6. Konosuke Kubo's hobby was collecting traditional handcrafted toys. According to Ms Hanai, there were paper kites from all over the country decorating the walls and hanging from the ceiling of the drawing and living rooms.

7. In his collection was a Yamaga lantern from Higo.

8. There were no specialist shops or department stores in the Tokyo area that sold or displayed Yamaga lanterns. (Asai had researched this himself after reading the report.) He had found department stores that had exhibited products from Kumamoto Prefecture or the Kyushu area, but none of them had ever displayed a Yamaga lantern.

9. Eiko's haiku had featured a Yamaga lantern. She must have seen it at Konosuke Kubo's house. In a separate haiku she had written about a Somin Shorai amulet. Asai presumed this was also part of Kubo's collection.

10. Ms Hanai had observed that Konosuke Kubo and Chiyoko Takahashi were only on the most basic of neighbourly terms, exchanging no more than greetings when they happened to meet. Ms Takahashi had never been inside Kubo's house.

That was it. Combine these ten separate pieces of data, and what other conclusion could be drawn?

According to her sister Miyako, Eiko had left home at one in the afternoon on 7 March. She must have gone to Kubo's house.

The maid, Ms Hanai, had told the investigator that she had three days off per month, but these were not on any set day of the week. Kubo mostly told her two or three days in advance when she wouldn't be needed. Obviously he was making sure that she wasn't around on the days when Eiko was visiting. Each time Kubo and Eiko met they probably made plans for their next meeting.

Elsewhere in the report, it was written that Kubo sometimes returned home from work in the middle of the day and let Ms Hanai leave early. These must also have been days that he was expecting Eiko. Three times a month on the maid's day off wasn't very often for a clandestine affair.

How had Eiko and Kubo met? He hadn't figured out that part of the puzzle yet. He'd have to hear that directly from Kubo. But that was beside the point. The result was all he really needed to consider.

In the beginning, Asai had believed his wife had gone to a couples' hotel with another man, even going so far as to ask at all three of the hotels on the top of the hill in Yoyogi, but now that he realized that she had been meeting her lover at the house where he lived alone, he saw how much more secure an arrangement that was. Unlike a hotel, there were no employees to see their faces, and no danger of running into other guests on the way in. It was a huge house with a garden separating it from the buildings on either side. You could make a lot of noise without anyone hearing you.

Ms Hanai had reported that there was one room in the house that she had not been permitted to clean. She'd thought it was the bedroom belonging to his wife up in the sanatorium in Nagano, but what if it had been the master bedroom? If that were the case, then it would contain either two single beds or one double bed. As Kubo's wife was away, who was using the other bed, or the other half of the double? Kubo must have cleaned that room himself. Ms Hanai had wrongly suspected that it contained some kind of valuable item that her client didn't want an employee to handle. But that wasn't the case – Kubo obviously didn't want the maid to discover what he'd been up to in there.

At first, Asai found it very hard to imagine Eiko going to Kubo's house. He knew her in the role of wife, but the Eiko who was intimate with Kubo was not Eiko the wife but Eiko the woman. A woman he didn't know at all. A woman who had pleaded illness in order to refuse her husband's sexual advances, then once he got used to their sexless marriage, had broken the rules that she herself had laid down. And she'd gone outside the marriage to break them.

He tried to see her in this new light, but as she'd always been at home when he came back from work, it was impossible to imagine. His personal experience of living with his wife was in total contrast to the unsavoury image in his head.

Was it his attempt to see things in a positive light? Or just the bravado of a man who didn't want to play the role of cuckolded husband?

As Asai now knew, at 3.25 p.m. on 7 March there had been an earthquake in Tokyo, one strong enough for objects to have fallen from shelves. A pre-war home such as Kubo's must have been shaken to its foundations. It was easy to picture one of the paper kites coming loose and falling on the gas heater. Normally there wouldn't have been any call for a heater in mid-afternoon in early March, but Asai had read a report that had mentioned a cold front passing through that day. The heater must have been on in order for the dislodged kite to have landed on the flame before falling.

Where in the house had Kubo and Eiko been at the time? What had they been doing? He didn't want to think about it. What he did know was the fire had been discovered relatively quickly and extinguished before it had done too much damage.

But how could Asai know for sure that his wife and Kubo were together at the time? The key was in the detective agency's report. The maid, Ms Hanai, had testified that she'd found three buckets, still wet, when she'd arrived the next day. For Asai, this was absolute proof.

A single person trying to extinguish a fire would use one bucket, or, at the most, two. In a state of panic, it's normal to fill one bucket and run towards the fire, emptying the water over the flames. But of course just one bucketful wouldn't be enough to extinguish it completely. The flames would recede momentarily but then flare up again, jumping to any places that hadn't been properly soaked. By yourself, you'd have to rush back to the water source, refill your bucket as quickly as possible, and then return to the fire. In your hurry you wouldn't have time to fill a second bucket – maybe half fill one at most?

But what if there were two people? While one person was throwing the water on the fire, the other could be filling a second bucket. And if they moved fast enough, it might even be possible to fill a third. A conveyor line with three buckets is impossible for only one person, but perfectly doable with two. Or maybe both people were throwing the water on the flames together. Only one tatami mat and part of one door partition had been burnt, so it seemed that two people working together had kept the fire from spreading.

That had to be it. Eiko had been right there in Konosuke Kubo's house when the fire broke out.

The sudden discovery of a fire in your living room – well, it'd be a shock to anyone. You'd panic. You'd have a vision of flames shooting through the roof as the house burned to the ground. Witnesses to a house fire have frequently testified that they have no memory of filling buckets and throwing them on the flames – that they moved in some sort of trance. The heart begins to pound, sending extra blood shooting through your veins; your breathing gets heavier, as if you're running up a steep hill.

That was it, thought Asai. That was when Eiko had had the heart attack.

Eiko's heart had been fragile, so much so that the doctor had advised her to avoid any excitement or shock that might affect it. And what greater trauma could there be than discovering a fire? Enough to deliver a shock even to someone with a healthy heart.

She'd done everything possible to protect her heart. She'd even asked for her husband's cooperation in avoiding the sex that might have harmed it. And that was how she'd gradually got him used to a life of abstinence.

But in the last few months she'd been in great health. She'd seemed no different from any normal, healthy person. In fact, it was as if she'd forgotten about her disease completely. Although she still had a weak heart, as long as nothing triggered an attack, it wasn't likely to affect her too much.

When she'd seen the fire her heart had been startled, and the resulting torrent of blood had flooded her coronary artery. But her blood vessels were fragile, and the flow had been blocked.

Eiko's reaction would also have had a psychological cause. She must have realized her predicament right away. Firefighters would arrive on the scene; there'd be crowds of onlookers. The police and firefighters would most probably question her after extinguishing the fire:

"Where were you, madam, when you noticed the fire?"

"And what were you doing at that time?"

"What is the exact nature of your relationship with Mr Konosuke Kubo?"

"When you say close friends, exactly how close do you mean?"

"So, madam, you only visited Mr Kubo's home on the housekeeper's day off, is that correct? Why did you visit him so often at a time which could so easily lead to misunderstandings?"

"Is your husband aware of the nature of your relationship?"

It was quite possible that these kinds of questions had been ringing in Eiko's ears.

And what of the gossips? There would be plenty of neighbours ready to speculate on the sight of a woman running from the burning house.

"Who's that?"

"It doesn't look like his wife."

"Of course it isn't – she's in a sanatorium up in Nagano. He lives alone these days."

"Oh, then that must be…"

As the flames had filled the living room and Eiko was hurriedly filling buckets with water from the kitchen tap, passing them to Kubo to throw on the fire, her head must have been spinning from these thoughts. Maybe she'd grabbed a bucket and run into the living room, raising it high in the air and hurling the water at the flames. Extreme physical exertion paired with extreme anxiety – could there have been anything more traumatic?

Suddenly there'd been a crippling pain in her heart. She'd collapsed to her knees, her skin soaked in a cold sweat. She'd shuddered in terror and begun to vomit.

He'd succeeded in putting out the fire, but what had Kubo's reaction been when he saw Eiko collapsed on the floor?

He'd been in no position to call a doctor. How would he explain the situation?

And how could he possibly let Eiko's family – in other words, her husband – know what had happened? Eiko had probably mentioned her husband to Kubo. Even if he'd never actually met him, he probably knew his name, his position at the ministry, maybe even their address and home telephone number. But even if he'd known all this, how on earth was he going to explain his reason for calling? How do you ask a man to come over to your house to pick up his wife's dead body?

Kubo also had to think of his own wife. She may have been in a sanatorium at the time, but she was likely to get wind of the events of that day at some point. No, she was bound to – after all, there had been a fire at her house and a strange woman in a state of distress. Kubo must have thought quickly. If he'd called a doctor, then the fire and the presence of his female companion would become known. The fire department would be alerted, and all the neighbours would hear about it. It would only have been a matter of time before someone told his wife.

There would have only been one possible course of action left to him – to cover up the whole thing. He'd got the idea of making it look as if Eiko had passed away somewhere other than this house. He couldn't carry her very far, so it would have to be somewhere nearby. It was reasonable to assume that was how she'd ended up at Chiyoko Takahashi's boutique.

According to the report, Konosuke Kubo and Chiyoko Takahashi were not close. They were no more than neighbours who occasionally exchanged greetings. But this was an emergency. He must have run, panicked, into her boutique, admitted that he had found himself in a very delicate situation and appealed to Ms Takahashi to help him. She would almost certainly have been alone in the shop at the time, and this would have made it possible for the two of them to concoct a plan that no one else would suspect.

Kubo's front garden was large, and raised above the road that passed in front. There was an embankment, topped with a bamboo fence, and then behind that some thick vegetation. In other words, the house was well concealed from any prying eyes. The house and the back entrance of Ms Takahashi's property were on the same high level, so it must have been relatively easy to transport Eiko that way without being seen.

At this point Eiko may already have been dead. No, she must have been, decided Asai. By the time Chiyoko Takahashi had told the university student to run and fetch Doctor Ohama, she was laid out in the tatami room at the back, no longer breathing.

"I checked my watch. It's very important to do that. It was 4.35 in the afternoon on the seventh of March… Her pupils were dilated and her heart had stopped beating. There was nothing I could do… According to Ms Takahashi, your wife had taken her last breath about thirty minutes before I arrived… And so I based the time of death on what Ms Takahashi told me… Probably not as long as an hour… Yes, well, I suppose it's possible…"

All Doctor Ohama's words. After persistent questioning by Asai, the doctor had finally conceded that Eiko could have passed away as long ago as an hour earlier.

Asai was certain that all of the evidence pointed to this being the reason that Kubo had signed over his land to Chiyoko Takahashi.

The Hotel Chiyo had appeared barely six months after Eiko's death. The negotiations must have begun right after the incident. How much had Ms Takahashi paid Kubo for his land?

Asai pictured the face of the cosmetics shop owner, her careful way of speaking and her engaging manner. But underneath lurked something not quite so pleasant – a greed and cunning, and the boldness that came with her thirty-something years. Perhaps she wasn't just the kept woman of the cosmetics wholesaler; what if they had conspired together to exploit Kubo's weakness?

Couples' hotels were a prosperous business. Up on that hill, all the hotels were thriving. He guessed that Ms Takahashi had long since given up on her failing cosmetics business and thought of going into the hotel business. And then suddenly there was a golden opportunity to acquire the land she needed. Kubo revealed his weakness when he asked for her help. She must have got an excellent price. It was blackmail, pure and simple. Certainly, Genkichi Higai must have been involved somehow. Or maybe they'd employed a yakuza type to threaten Kubo. Konosuke Kubo's name may only have been added to the list of board members for the sake of appearances.

To tell the truth, Asai wasn't all that interested in the exact method Ms Takahashi had used to get Kubo's land. He was far more interested in Kubo himself. The man who had killed his wife.

He could have investigated whether the days of Eiko's excursions corresponded with Kubo's days off work, or the days he'd left work early, but he didn't really need to.

Back at the ministry, Asai scrutinized documents, met with manufacturers and businessmen, attended meetings, drafted proposals. But in every quiet moment his mind was assaulted by the image of the tall man with the long face.

13

The detective agency's report had mentioned that on the last Saturday of the month, Konosuke Kubo used to travel by train up to a sanatorium on the Fujimi plateau to visit his wife. He always took the train nicknamed Alps #4, which left Shinjuku Station at 1.10 p.m. Asai found this last part out himself by calling R-Textiles one Saturday afternoon and telling the receptionist in General Affairs that he was an acquaintance of Kubo's.

"I'm sorry – Mr Kubo left about an hour ago. Yes, he's on his way to Fujimi in Nagano Prefecture… Which train? The 1.10 express from Shinjuku… Yes, that's right. He always takes that one."

It took about three and a half hours to get from Shinjuku to Fujimi. Kubo would be getting in around 5 p.m. That would fit in nicely with visiting hours at the sanatorium. Asai imagined that he would stay the night in Fujimi or neighbouring Kamisuwa, then go back again to the sanatorium on Sunday morning to spend some more time with his wife before returning to Tokyo.

Visiting Nagano once a month without fail to comfort his sick wife made Kubo look like a caring husband, but Asai was sure that he felt obliged to do it for show. This was the same man who had thought only of saving his own skin when he dragged Eiko's dead body to Chiyoko Takahashi's shop. Everything was appearances with him – he was cunning and two-faced.

The fourth Saturday in October fell on the twenty-fifth.

A little before one in the afternoon, Asai was walking along the Chuo Line platform at Shinjuku, his dark glasses in place. The Alps #4 was already sitting in the station, allowing him to walk the full length of the train, glancing into the windows with an air of nonchalance. Kubo wouldn't recognize his face, which gave Asai a distinct advantage when tailing him.

Kubo was sitting in the first-class car, around the middle of the carriage, next to the left-hand window. He was reading a newspaper. There was no one next to him and one older gentleman sitting opposite. The two men appeared not to know each other. Asai seated himself several rows away, across from a mother and child, but kept Kubo in sight.

Seeing as Asai knew Kubo's destination, he wouldn't need to observe him the whole time. However, he had one small concern. This express didn't stop at Fujimi station. According to the timetable, it would stop at the slightly larger Kobuchizawa, just before Fujimi, at 4.24 p.m. They would need to transfer to a local train, departing at 4.52 and arriving at Fujimi at 5.05. There would be about a thirty-minute wait on the platform at Kobuchizawa.

Would Kubo wait there for half an hour, or would he just take a taxi directly to the sanatorium? It was difficult to predict, although Asai thought the taxi would be the more sensible of the two options.

Asai planned to confront Kubo somewhere en route to the sanatorium. Visiting hours were probably limited, so he could conceivably catch him on his way out, but it would be getting late by then. If, say, visiting hours ended at eight, it would already be dark, and he wasn't sure that Kubo would be willing to talk to him. Ideally, he should try to intercept him in a quiet location, with no one around.

So it was going to be important to keep an eye on Kubo, just in case he didn't get off the train at Kobuchizawa after all. He'd assumed at first that the man would go straight to Fujimi, but what if he didn't? What if he'd just told everyone that he visited his wife from Saturday to Sunday, but in fact spent the Saturday night enjoying himself at a completely different location before turning up at the sanatorium on Sunday? He might spend the night at the hot-spring resort of Kofu, or even somewhere further afield, such as Shimosuwa.

The train set off. Kubo was still reading his newspaper, and hadn't met or spoken to anyone. Asai tried to read a magazine, but it was hopeless; the letters wouldn't stay still on the page.

A large number of passengers got off at Kofu. Other groups of sightseers boarded, apparently on their way to admire the autumn leaves. There were signboards on the platform touting the beauty of the Shosenkyo Gorge at this time of year. Asai raised his head to check on Kubo. He hadn't moved from his seat and was staring out of the window, smoking a cigarette. He looked bored.

So he would either get off at Kobuchizawa or Shimosuwa. If it was Kobuchizawa, would he wait thirty minutes on the platform for the local train, or take a taxi?

After Kofu, the train slowed down as it began to climb more steeply. The outline of Mount Fuji disappeared

146

from the left-side window just as the mountain ridge of Yatsugatake became visible on the right. The woods on both sides became gradually more crimson.

With all the new passengers from Kofu, half the carriage was filled with new faces. The elderly gentleman opposite Kubo had been replaced by an elegant woman of around thirty, dressed in a kimono. Asai wondered whether the two had planned to meet on the train, and watched the movement of their heads over the top of the seats, but they didn't appear to be talking to one another. They must be strangers, after all. Kubo seemed to be engrossed in some kind of magazine now.

This was the first time that Asai had ever had the chance to observe the object of his hostility for such a long period of time. He watched his every gesture: the turn of his head, his hand movements, the hunch of his shoulders – everything typical of the average Joe, bored by a long train journey. When he thought of how his own wife could have been seduced by a blend of such banal and trivial gestures, he felt something grow in the pit of his stomach and the bile began to rise in his throat. But along with the unpleasantness, there was a sweet feeling of satisfaction that all his efforts to discover the identity of his rival had led to this moment. In order to completely savour the sensation, he would have to take care how he went about the next stage of his plan.

Asai hadn't loved Eiko to the extent that his heart would never recover from the shock of her death. What he felt now was anger that she had betrayed him, and that the coldness that she had shown him was the fault of this man, Kubo. He couldn't let things be. He hated this man whose seduction techniques had reignited a spark in his wife after she'd been frigid for so many years. He knew that Kubo was capable of all kinds of cunning and ingenuity, as evidenced by his plan to dump Eiko's body on his neighbour. Asai's thoughts were not of avenging his poor wife for having been innocently led astray by this playboy; no, this revenge was entirely for himself. At least, if he'd stopped and thought about it, that was the conclusion he would have come to, but in the heat of the moment he was blinded by his emotions and had convinced himself that he was there to vindicate Eiko.

The train crossed the border into Nagano Prefecture, and immediately began to slow even more. Passengers began to stand and gather their belongings. The tall figure of Kubo rose from his seat and reached for his bag from the overhead luggage rack. Asai sprang to attention. It was just as he'd thought – he planned to get off at Kobuchizawa.

As the train pulled into the station, Kubo set off for the far exit door, without once glancing back. Asai immediately exited from the other end of the carriage.

Around half of the passengers headed straight for the steps up to the exit bridge, and the rest stayed on the platform to wait for the local train. Kubo was among the twenty or so who stayed. The train would get him to Fujimi in under fifteen minutes, so Asai supposed it was worth waiting the extra half hour to save on the taxi fare. He was sure Kubo felt no pressing need to rush to his sick wife's bedside.

Asai kept himself at a safe distance. Kubo was facing east, so Asai made sure he was turned the opposite way. Across from him was a tall mountain, whose name he didn't know. The late-afternoon sun shone crimson on its summit. It was the end of October, and the air was rather cold so high up. Standing completely alone, your shadow thrown across an unknown station platform by the setting sun, would have been enough to make anyone melancholy, but Asai didn't feel any sadness right at that moment.

It was a long half hour, but the train finally came. There weren't many people boarding, so Asai made sure he chose a different carriage. As the train passed through the ridge, the mountains cast a bluish shadow over the autumn colours, and beyond, the far slopes of Yatsugatake were pitch-black.

Kubo was among the passengers getting off at Fujimi. Asai imagined his bulging bag was filled with presents for his sick wife. He followed him, making sure there were no more than three or four other people between them at any time. He feared losing sight of the man, and even more that Kubo might take a taxi from the rank in front of the station. If that looked likely, Asai intended to approach him before he could climb in.

But to Asai's surprise Kubo got on to a bus that was waiting in front of the station. He hadn't prepared for that eventuality, but he decided it would be safe to get on too. Asai would just have to make sure he kept his back to Kubo all the way to the stop for the sanatorium.

They passed by the bright lights around the station, and headed out of the town. Up on the expanse of the plateau, small glimmers of daylight remained. Kubo got off at the sanatorium, followed by three other passengers. Asai hung back.

About fifty yards away, built on the highest ground, the sanatorium, with its brightly lit windows, looked just like a hotel. The three passengers who had got off the bus in front of him turned off in different directions, so at last Asai was alone with Kubo in the midst of this vast landscape.

The other man set off along the road. Asai raised his dark glasses to look at his watch. It was just before six. Kubo's slightly hunched figure was a few yards in front of him. The road sloped upwards. As a car headed towards them from the direction of the sanatorium, Asai turned his face away from the glare of its headlights.

After the car had passed, Asai called out to Kubo.

"Excuse me!" His voice came out breathless. He didn't sound like himself at all.

The figure ahead stopped and turned. In the gloom he could just make out the long, bespectacled face. It was definitely the same man who'd been watching him outside the cosmetics boutique. But this time he seemed less menacing. He could see at once that Kubo didn't recognize him, and this gave him a slight sense of relief, but at the same time his heart lurched in his chest.

This lasted a mere two or three seconds, then Asai approached Kubo, a smile on his face.

"Excuse me, but are you Mr Kubo?" This time his voice came out normally.

"Yes, that's right."

Kubo stood there looking a little puzzled, apparently waiting to discover who this was addressing him.

"Are you on your way to the sanatorium?"

"Yes, but… If you don't mind my asking, who are you?"

Asai stood his ground. The other man being much taller than he was, he was forced to raise his eyes to look him in the face.

"I'm Asai."

Kubo looked even more puzzled. He hadn't realized who Asai was. He was clearly trying to recall all the Asais of his acquaintance.

"I'm sorry, Mr Asai from...?"

"Tsuneo Asai. Surely this isn't the first time you've heard my name?"

It was a dramatic way to announce it, but he hadn't prepared for this particular conversation, so it just came out that way.

Kubo suddenly looked as though he had swallowed a lump of lead. His glasses had slipped a little way down his nose, but his eyes were fixed firmly on Asai's face. Asai continued.

"No, in fact, this is the first time we've met. I'm Eiko's husband, Tsuneo Asai."

Asai spoke frankly, and even bowed his head slightly.

"Mr Kubo, I'd like to ask you some questions about my wife. Could you spare me some time?" he asked, raising his eyes once again to Kubo's.

A look of panic crossed Kubo's face. If it hadn't been so dark, Asai was sure he'd have seen his features twisting and his eyes blinking rapidly. He was yet to reply.

"You're just about to visit your wife, I presume." Asai took another step forward. "I'm sure you're in a hurry, so shall we just have a chat in the lobby or the waiting room?"

"No," interrupted Kubo. "Not there. It's impossible."

"I see. That'd be a problem for you, would it?"

"Yes. Please spare me that." Kubo was almost begging.

"I see. You don't want your wife asking awkward questions?"

"Right." Kubo hung his head.

"I understand. Well then, where shall we have our conversation? It's already getting late and dark…"

Kubo didn't respond.

"There don't seem to be any cafés around here. Is there a coffee shop or something at the sanatorium?"

"I'd prefer to avoid any of those places," said Kubo weakly.

"So where can we talk? Should we go back to town? Wait for the next bus?"

"No… no. If you don't mind, could we go for a walk somewhere? I'd rather not have anyone overhear our conversation."

"Take a walk? You mean on one of these country roads?"

Kubo bowed his head in supplication. "Yes. If that's all right."

To tell the truth, this was what Asai had hoped for all along. Or it would be more accurate to say he had steered events directly towards this outcome.

What Asai had never anticipated was that Kubo would admit so easily to his relationship with Eiko. He'd expected his adversary to play dumb, to deny everything. After all, the man had shown himself to be a wily character. Asai had expected to have to work to get any kind of confession, and had come prepared for all different lines of attack. But he hadn't needed any. Kubo hadn't dodged his questions, presumably because Asai had managed to take him by surprise, to materialize right in front of him out of the darkness. He had been unable to defend himself. Overwhelmed by his accuser's determined manner, Kubo had realized that Asai knew the whole truth.

The two men turned off the road to the sanatorium and took what was barely more than a track towards the foot of the Yatsugatake mountain ridge. There were few buildings in sight, and just the odd light vaguely visible between the dark mass of the forest and the smaller groves of trees. There was nobody else around.

Kubo, suitcase in hand, looked as if he were being frogmarched by Asai along the narrow, faintly luminescent trail. Throwing furtive glances at his guard as he walked, he was clearly afraid of what Asai might say or do to him next. He reminded Asai of a weakened, trapped animal, looking for a chance to escape.

Good. In that case, I'll leave him to sweat a bit more before I ask him any more questions, thought Asai. It reminded him of being back at the ministry, taking advantage of the weaker status of some businessman just to keep him waiting.

The two walked about fifty yards along the track, each deep in thought. It was Kubo who stopped first.

"Mr Asai."

It was the voice of someone who desperately needed to break the silence.

14

"Mr Asai," repeated Kubo, his voice low. They stood on the dark track, Kubo looking down at Asai. "Please say what you came to say."

Asai felt the bite of the frosty air on his cheeks; the temperature up here in the mountains was like late November in the city. The cold seeped through his layers of clothing and chilled his back. He looked around.

"I see. No one around here to overhear our conversation."

The sanatorium wasn't visible from where they stood. The Yatsugatake ridge formed a towering, black wall that blocked their view. Nothing was visible besides the scattering of lights that seemed to cascade down the base of the ridge. One side of the track was thickly wooded; on the other, beyond a narrow area of scrub, fields stretched away steeply into the distance. There was a scent of dried grass in the air.

"Mr Asai, what's all this about?"

"I want to know what happened the day Eiko died. That's what I've come to ask you about."

Kubo's shoe made a small crunching sound on the gravel track.

"The day she died? I've no idea. How would I know anything about that?"

"And yet you and Eiko were on very intimate terms."

Kubo didn't reply.

"There's no point in trying to deny it. Just now, when I told you I was Eiko's husband, didn't you panic and lead me away from the sanatorium and all the way out to the middle of nowhere just to talk? If you weren't involved with Eiko, why would you behave this way?"

"I'm not saying I didn't know her. I'm not denying it, but… Is that why you followed me all the way up here?"

"I didn't follow you. I just created an opportunity for us to talk. I couldn't just turn up at your office, or pay a visit to your apartment. That would have been incredibly humiliating for me."

"So you knew that I'd be coming to this sanatorium."

"Every fourth Saturday of the month you come here to visit your wife. I have my ways of finding out, Mr Kubo. I've already discovered quite a lot about you. I know all about you and Eiko. But I want to hear it directly from your own mouth. Ideally, I would have asked my wife to tell me herself, but unfortunately she can't because she's dead. You're the only one who can tell me the truth."

"Didn't Eiko – I mean, your wife – tell you anything before she died?"

"I think you know perfectly well that she didn't. If she had done, I'm sure she would have told you about it. Eiko used to visit you twice a week at your old home in Yoyogi, didn't she?"

Kubo made a movement. For a moment, Asai thought he was going to run for it, but he simply turned and stared out across the fields. Far off on the horizon, through a gap between the mountains, a tiny patch of starry sky was visible. Kubo placed his suitcase on the ground and got a packet of cigarettes out of his pocket. It felt as if he was playing for time. The lenses of his glasses and the end of his nose were briefly lit by the orange flame of his cigarette lighter, and then were instantly gone as the lighter clicked off. After that there was nothing but the tiny red glow of his cigarette. He exhaled smoke into the air, but made no move to speak.

"It seems you're having trouble coming up with a response, so shall I get it started for you?" said Asai with a sneer. Kubo nervously drew on his cigarette.

"All right, then. Mr Kubo, Eiko wrote all about you and your relationship in her private diaries. I found them in a locked drawer after she died. She wrote about every single visit she paid to your house. I assume that if she ever planned to commit suicide, or found herself sick and close to death, she would have got rid of the books. But as she died suddenly, away from home, she never got the chance. The whole affair is laid out in those diaries."

Still, Kubo said nothing.

"You have an interest in folk arts and crafts, don't you? Kites and dolls and things? Wood carvings and stuff made out of paper, right? In your collection, you have a Yamaga lantern from Kumamoto Prefecture. And a Somin Shorai amulet. Eiko thought these things were unusual and interesting, and wrote about them in her diary."

Kubo shuddered slightly, as if the cold night air had suddenly invaded his body.

"But there's one thing I don't know. How did you two become close? That was the only thing her diary didn't mention. It sounded as if at the start she was a little afraid to write, and she left that part out. How and where did you first meet?"

Kubo threw away his cigarette, half-smoked.

"All right. I'll tell you. It'll explain why I don't owe you any kind of apology."

His tall frame turned once again to face Asai.

"I admit that Eiko and I were lovers. It began about two years ago. We met at an old temple in Fuchu. I'd heard that they sold Somin Shorai amulets and had gone to buy one. Eiko was there, walking in the temple grounds. The grounds were otherwise deserted – it was a very quiet place. I ended up speaking to her. Eiko told me she was there to get inspiration for her haiku."

Asai knew that Eiko had often made trips to various places in Tokyo and its suburbs to find inspiration for her poems. However, he had never guessed that this was how her relationship with Kubo had begun. He'd had all kinds of theories about their first meeting, but he had never expected it to have been pure chance.

"That day, the two of us walked about a mile back to the station together chatting about this and that, and then, about a week later, I ran into her again – this time in a department store in Shinjuku. I got on the escalator to go up to the first floor, and she was standing one step below me."

Asai guessed that coincidences like this one would strengthen the bond between two people. They went and had lunch together at a nearby restaurant. Kubo explained that they had such a good time talking that they planned to meet again the following week.

"If Eiko wrote about me in her diary, then I can't deny it. I don't know what she wrote exactly, but let's say I confirm everything that she said about us."

Kubo blurted this out, and then started over in a more measured tone.

"That said, I don't want you to misunderstand my motives. In the beginning, Eiko never told me that she was married. She said she was still single."

Asai gasped.

"I only slept with Eiko because she told me she wasn't married. How could I have done something like that if I'd known from the start that there was a husband in the picture? I was completely convinced that she was a single woman who'd somehow missed the boat on the marriage thing. Do you get it, Mr Asai? I was deceived by Eiko, just like you were."

Asai was left speechless.

"Eiko finally told me the truth after we'd been together about a year. She cried when she admitted it, and – I have to tell you – I was horrified. But it was already too late. I was too involved with her to end things. She said that she had deceived me and she'd understand if I wanted to break it off, but that she wanted from the bottom of her heart to keep on seeing me. And that was how our love affair continued. That's the truth, Mr Asai. I never stole another man's wife away from him. I slept with Eiko believing that she was unattached. If I'd known she was your wife then I would have been guilty of adultery, and I'd owe you an apology. I'd be morally to blame. But I didn't know. I was tricked. And so I've no intention of getting down on my knees to ask forgiveness. I mean, I suppose what I did after

Eiko had confessed the truth wasn't exactly blameless – we did continue our affair for another year – but Eiko begged me in tears not to let her husband find out. I just got caught up and dragged along with the whole thing, and that's the truth."

Kubo had told the whole story without a pause. He'd latched onto the excuse "From the beginning Eiko told me she was single" and based all of his logic around it. It sounded as if he'd constructed himself a fine argument. He'd regained all of his self-confidence. He was even beginning to sound aggressive.

Asai was sure he was lying. He was convinced that Kubo had seduced Eiko. And that Eiko had told him from the outset that she was married. With someone like Kubo, it probably added to the attraction that he was toying with someone else's wife. And now he was employing his usual cunning to talk Asai into believing the exact opposite. No doubt he'd been silent during their walk up here because he was busy concocting this cock and bull story.

"So I'm to understand that you think you owe me no kind of apology whatsoever?" asked Asai, his tone rather less calm than before.

Kubo glanced around him as if to check no one was around on the remote track. But Asai also guessed that Kubo felt confident because he was a few years younger and rather bigger than his adversary.

"I don't believe that I need to answer to anything. I'm nothing but the innocent victim of Eiko's deceit. An apology is something you offer when you're guilty of something, okay? Right then, say that for the sake of argument what Eiko and I did was adultery; you do realize that adultery is no longer illegal? Not even the law recognizes it as a crime any more. To say nothing of the fact that, as I've already said, I began sleeping with Eiko because she told me she wasn't married. It doesn't make any difference that she told me later – the responsibility is all hers!"

"So you don't feel any moral responsibility to me at all?"

"I object to being forced to say it! I feel sorry for you, of course I do. But when somebody tails me all the way up to Nagano and gets me out into the middle of nowhere in the pitch dark just to intimidate me and extort some kind of apology, well… even if I was feeling like apologizing at one time, I certainly don't feel like it any more!"

"I see. Well, the only reason I followed you up here is that in Tokyo there is nowhere we could have this conversation. I already mentioned that. You complain that we're in the pitch darkness in the middle of nowhere, but it's because your train got in at this time. And it was you who chose a country road to have a conversation. I suggested we go and talk inside the sanatorium, but you were the one who told me it was impossible. You brought me out here, not the other way round."

"That's right. Because you threatened to have this conversation in front of my wife. So tell me – what exactly are you after?"

"After?"

"Well, I don't imagine you've come all the way up here just to intimidate me into getting down on hands and knees and begging your forgiveness. There's more to it than that, isn't there?"

"Ha!" Asai stepped so far forward that Kubo must have felt his breath on his face. "I'd say you have plenty of other reasons besides me to feel intimidated."

"What are you talking about?"

"Chiyoko Takahashi and the house in Yoyogi that she took from you. Yes, I found out just about everything from my investigations. Ha! It's pointless to try to look so innocent. You asked your neighbour, Ms Takahashi, to help you get rid of my poor wife's body after she died in your house, because you couldn't face handing over her dead body to my family yourself. So to save your own reputation, instead of finding some empty land somewhere to dump her corpse, you had the brilliant idea of asking the owner of the cosmetics shop next door to deal with it. You came up with the story that Eiko had been walking in the street when she had suddenly felt ill and stumbled into a nearby cosmetics boutique, where she'd then passed away. Easy to believe it of someone like you – a man obsessed with appearances and with the morals of a snake. Getting a woman you barely know to agree so easily to such a sordid plan – well, you dug your own grave there, didn't you? Chiyoko Takahashi turned out to be tougher than you thought. She took advantage of your dilemma and got your house and its plot of land for a bargain-basement price. But blackmail on this level must have been a collaboration. I know she had a hand from her patron – a certain wholesaler in the cosmetics trade. I'm not just making this stuff up. I hired a private detective to look into your business. These ex-police officers really know their stuff. Ms Takahashi spilled the beans about everything. She didn't actually admit to having blackmailed you, but it was pretty clear from what she told them. Here you go – this is the report of their findings, in case you're interested."

Asai produced the envelope from his jacket pocket, and pulled the pages halfway out to reveal some of the printed words. The white sheets of paper reflected the little bit of light out there on the track.

Kubo stiffened. The appearance of the detective agency's report from its manila envelope seemed to have dealt him quite a blow. He didn't even have the energy to take a look at its contents and check if Asai was telling the truth. It must have been a shock to hear that Chiyoko Takahashi had admitted the whole thing to a private detective.

"And the detectives also paid a visit to Komako Hanai. She gave them quite a lot of information as well. Komako Hanai – you remember her, right? The woman the maid service used to send to your house? The detective agency really did its job there. She'd quit the maid service and gone to live in the remotest part of Yamanashi Prefecture, but they managed to track her down, just to get her to talk to them."

This was another blow that Kubo wasn't expecting. It may have just been the cold, but his whole body was shivering. He stood, rooted to the spot, as Asai continued. About the *fusuma* doors and the tatami that had burned in the 7 March earthquake; how Ms Hanai had mentioned that Kubo had used three buckets to put out the fire. He reconstructed the housekeeper's account, and added how Eiko must have collapsed from the mixture of emotional shock and physical trauma.

"You had no idea that Eiko had heart trouble, did you? Apparently, she didn't confide in you about everything. She acted as if she didn't know that she was ill, and went about her life normally, but in fact she was afraid to tell you about it, in case it scared you off. The one thing that was most dangerous for her weak heart was sex. But somehow she ended up so infatuated with you that she forgot all about that. You as good as killed Eiko yourself. In fact, what you did could be considered a criminal act."

"Wha—"

"You transported a dead body, without due cause, to the house of an unrelated third party. I believe that's enough to charge you with abandonment of a corpse."

Kubo stamped his foot in fury.

"What the hell are you after? You're no better than that Takahashi woman with your threats! What is it you want from me? Money?"

He was bellowing now.

"Money, is it? Yeah, I bet it is!"

"Not money."

"Liar! Your whole plan was to follow me here and extort cash from me. But you're not going to get one over on me that easily. I've got a little countermeasure that I can put into play."

"A countermeasure?"

"Exactly. If you go ahead with this, I'm going to tell my wife everything. Chiyoko Takahashi has already cheated me out of my home; I've nothing more to fear. I heard from Eiko that you're a section chief at the Ministry of Agriculture and Forestry. A senior civil servant at a government ministry using his own wife's adultery to blackmail someone? That's an abuse of power, and it reeks of some kind of scam."

Asai was brought up as abruptly as if he had collided with a boulder in the dark.

"It's very funny to me," continued Kubo. "Me – a lowly salaryman in my uncle's modest company. Really, none of this would have any effect on my reputation. My uncle's not going to fire me. It looks like my wife has lung cancer, so she's not long for this world. In other words, I really don't have anything left to lose. You, on the other hand… If I brought a complaint against you for attempted blackmail… well, you wouldn't be able to function as a civil servant any longer. I mean, I suppose you'd be able to continue until the result of the trial, but I'm sure they'd make you give up your position as section chief. But no, before it even got to that point, the gutter press – those weekly 'news magazines' – would be all over the story. You wouldn't dare even show your face at work again, because you wouldn't want to appear with egg on it in front of all those bosses and superiors you've been kowtowing to all these years."

What Tsuneo Asai had in common with all other non-career-track civil servants who had fought their way up to their positions was a fierce sense of pride, and loyalty to his own ministry, where he would do anything to hold on to his job. Now that his position was threatened, a powerful instinct for self-preservation kicked in. And that was the motive for what happened next.

Asai was aided and abetted by the heavy darkness of the Fujimi plateau.

15

Asai had no memory of how he'd got from the track back on to the main road.

The night enveloped him. It felt heavy, weighted. It was as if he were walking through deep water; the air was resisting him and his legs wouldn't move the way he wanted them to. He had to force a path through the darkness. The woods and forest to the side of the road were vibrating. It was like a scene from a dark fairy tale, with the faint lights from distant habitations barely making it through the swirling fog.

But Asai didn't feel the cold; his whole body felt on fire. He was acutely aware of his own ragged breathing – his exhaled breath seemed to heat the air around him.

In his mind, the thing he had just done was already disconnecting itself from reality. He hadn't willed it to happen; it wasn't premeditated, nor was it a dream he'd long held. He'd done it on impulse. His brain hadn't engaged, and his hand had seemed to move all by itself. In that moment, all ties to his consciousness had been severed.

The small bottle of acid had been hidden in his pocket the whole time, but he'd never really intended to use it as a weapon. Konosuke Kubo was younger than him and well-built. Asai had merely thought that if the conversation had deteriorated into a fight, he would be ready. If the physically stronger Kubo came at him, he planned to throw the contents of the bottle at him to make him back off. And that would give Asai the chance to run away. He'd put the acid into an empty bottle he'd found among Eiko's things. It used to contain her favourite brand of hair oil. It was a small, elegant-looking bottle with a gold-coloured lid and silver label. He'd filled it with acid, pushed the stopper in tightly and then screwed the lid shut.

When Kubo had threatened to sue Asai for blackmail, Asai had thought that his career as a civil servant was over. He'd never expected this turn of events. It had filled him with confusion and terror. He'd imagined Kubo prostrate before him, bowing his head to the dirt a thousand times and confessing his wrongdoing in a desperate, choking voice. His immediate goal was to be able to look down on his trembling adversary as he begged for Asai's mercy and forgiveness. But he'd thought no further than this immediate objective – in other words, he hadn't planned what to do next. Once he had Kubo down on his hands and knees he'd envisaged being free to humiliate the man at his leisure. Asai had never imagined any other outcome besides being able to watch Kubo become more and more pathetic. He'd expected to have been in a position to suggest more ways for Kubo to abase himself and he'd been looking forward to watching him do it.

Kubo's counterattack had been sudden and more brutal than Asai could ever have imagined. He had gone straight for the Achilles heel, and Asai was floored. The ministry was the one place where this affair could never be known about. Of course, Kubo could have been bluffing, but Asai couldn't risk being exposed to the judgement of his superiors. It was vital to Asai that his colleagues never heard the voice of this wounded beast ranting and raging. The truth is that the explosion in Asai's head was ignited by his instinct for self-preservation.

It had been a great struggle to pass the entrance examination to become a civil servant. Then, once in, he had hoisted himself, rung by rung, up the ladder to where he was now. By the time he realized that it was completely pointless to rage against the absurdity and the inequality of the elitist system, he'd already made up his mind to compete against the elite by performing the work better than they ever could. He worked harder than anyone else and spent longer hours in the office. He'd spent the first ten or more years of his working life subjected to scorn and sarcasm. He studied all the rules and regulations down to the fine print, sacrificed any kind of private life to fact-finding investigations of all aspects of the manufacturing industry. The result of all this hard slog was that he was known as "The Demon" or "The Walking Encyclopaedia" of the staple foods division, and even his division chief and director respected and counted on him. He had great authority over the manufacturers – they considered him the *éminence grise* of the division and were intimidated by him. If he was your ally, you could ask him anything, but – rumour had it – make an enemy of him and he would be a fearsome opponent, not only of the manufacturers but within the ministry too. This hard-won reputation would crumble if Konosuke Kubo were to blab.

And then *it* happened…

His whole career flashed before his eyes – everything he'd done since entering the Ministry of Agriculture and Forestry. The faces of the superiors who terrified him when he was a new employee; the books of laws and regulations that he'd relentlessly read, and read again, until he had memorized every last page, and how it had felt when he could reveal to his bosses his vast knowledge of legislation; his pride when he saw the look on the face of his division chief the first time he had expressed an opinion on a complicated issue; the respect he got from the president of Yagishita Ham and the other veteran manufacturers; every event that had contributed to his increase in confidence and rise in rank to respected employee. A succession of images sped through his head, much in the way they say images from your childhood flash before your eyes right before you die.

Asai took the bottle from his pocket. Under cover of darkness, he unscrewed the gold lid and carefully removed the stopper. Kubo, in his fury, had no idea what was happening. Asai waited until the tall figure of his adversary leaned in towards him, and then jerked the bottle upwards, drawing a semicircle in the air with his arm. In the dark, the stream of liquid that came flying out was invisible, but he heard the scream. The silhouette of the man before him clutched his hands to his face and collapsed to a crouching position.

Squatting on the bare earth, Kubo fumbled madly in his pockets for a handkerchief and pressed it to his eyes. He didn't get up again. Uncanny sounds came out of him, like the mewling of a newborn baby. His body spun around and around as he made to get up and then crumpled back down again. He looked like a dancer in a child's music box, although he never once removed the handkerchief from his eyes.

Then he began to yell.

"Run to the sanatorium and get me an ambulance! My eyes are melting. They're melting! My face is burning. That's all I ask – get me an ambulance. I'm going blind. My eyes are melting – they're running down my face! Please do something!"

Kubo howled and sobbed, his voice no longer human.

Asai realized some drops of the acid must have got in his eyes. He hadn't mixed it with any water – it was neat sulphuric acid. He'd gone all the way to a chemist's in Shinagawa, a part of Tokyo far enough from his home, claiming he needed it to unblock a toilet.

But how could he just leave his enemy here like this? Kubo's eyes might be destroyed, but his mouth still worked. He could still do a lot of damage to Asai.

"All right. Just wait a minute while I fetch someone," he said reassuringly. Checking there was no one coming, he began to feel around for a hefty stone.

When the first rock came down on his head, Kubo's shriek tore through the darkness, and he collapsed face down in the dirt. The white handkerchief slipped from his grasp and fluttered gently to the ground, but his hand didn't move.

Asai wasn't foolish enough to pick up the same rock that he had just used to hit Kubo – it would be splattered all over with the man's blood. It wouldn't do to get it all over his sleeves or the front of his clothes. He went in search of a second stone. This time he didn't need to tell Kubo to wait for him.

Kubo lay on the ground, the rocks next to his head, a snake that had just been battered to death with three stones. Asai felt strangely calm. His principal emotion was that of relief: he'd managed to stop his enemy from talking. He gave Kubo's leg a kick just to check. It moved a little way and then stopped – an inanimate object. Neither his head nor his body showed any signs of movement.

Looking more closely at the man's face, Asai was surprised to see that there was nothing visible of Kubo's features. Darkened with blood, his face blended into the shadows. Only the three rocks, in their triangular formation around his head, gleamed faintly in the darkness.

He turned and felt the oppressive presence of the Yatsugatake ridge looming over him. As he realized that he had done something irrevocable, a wave of intense heat spread through his whole body. He had become a killer, and it had taken only five minutes. He had never once imagined that this would be his destiny. It really didn't suit him; the self he was familiar with would never be able to kill another person. It wasn't in his nature; he must have accidentally let an object fall from his hand…

Asai set off along the main prefectural route in the direction of the station, or at least the direction he thought it was. He'd gone a dozen paces or so when he halted abruptly. All the hair on his body suddenly stood on end. He'd left the hair oil bottle lying there on the ground.

Should he go back and pick it up? If he went back to where the corpse lay and happened to meet someone – even if he got the bottle and only happened to pass somebody on his way back – and they got a look at his face, a few days later his identikit picture might end up as an important clue in the investigation.

He looked around him. No vehicles or pedestrians in sight. Even this prefectural highway (or at least that was what Asai assumed it was) was utterly deserted. So there was even less reason to think there might be anyone on one of the minor turn-offs into the mountains. Still, it really wasn't safe to assume anything; the worst luck can hit you at the most unexpected of moments.

In the end he decided to leave it. It was a pretty common brand of hair oil, made in Japan. Eiko had generally had expensive tastes, but this particular range, made by S-Pharmaceuticals, wasn't one of the more exclusive imported brands. They must sell bottles of this product in the tens of thousands every day all over Japan. On top of that, the bottle he'd used was an old one that Eiko had already emptied. She must have bought it over a year ago, somewhere in Tokyo. He'd examined it closely before filling it with the acid; it had no distinguishing characteristics, and the label was quite worn.

And anyway, this was Nagano Prefecture. If the police decided to use the bottle as a clue, they'd start by questioning people in the neighbourhood. Just because the victim was from Tokyo, there was no reason to assume that he had been followed here by someone with the intention of murdering him. He didn't expect the investigating officers to ask S-Pharmaceuticals about their sales of hair oil right off the bat. And when they did, he was sure when they heard how many millions of bottles had been sold in the many thousands of shops all over the country, the officer in charge would have no option other than to thank them and take his leave.

No, there was no point in letting the seeds of doubt put down roots in his mind. Better to dig them out right away.

But he wasn't completely out of danger yet; the unexpected could happen. If he ran into someone, for example, he'd be done for. Best to get the hell out of there as fast as possible.

Asai was horrified to find himself thinking this way. Wasn't this the way a murderer would think? Even without a plan, even though it hadn't happened of his own free will, there was no doubt that he had committed a crime. A perfectly normal wave had suddenly upended him at the water's edge, and before he knew it his whole body had been dragged out to the open sea. Had it been the result of carelessness, or a mistake? Whatever the case, he felt as if he had been swallowed up by a huge, dark wave of absurdity. He had been controlled by the exterior forces of nature.

He was able to describe his feelings in this way, but Asai still hadn't acknowledged to himself that he was guilty. He was dissatisfied by the outcome; it wasn't at all what he had set out to achieve. For example, had his intention been to kill Kubo, he'd have felt some measure of satisfaction just from having tried, even if he'd failed. But is there any satisfaction to be gained from killing someone on impulse? Apparently not.

This wasn't about avenging Eiko after all. If he'd been after revenge for her death, there was no need to go that far. He realized he hadn't been that deeply in love with her. There was no call to commit a grievous crime in the name of a woman you didn't truly love. All he'd have needed to heal the wound of Eiko's betrayal would have been the heartfelt apology of the man she had betrayed him with. If Kubo had just thrown himself to his knees in the middle of that country road and rubbed his forehead in the dirt, begging Asai's pardon, then nothing bad would have happened. He'd hoped for no more than that. He would have been perfectly satisfied.

Kubo should never have gone on the attack. Driven into a corner, he had suddenly leapt back up, his claws out. If there was anything that Asai regretted, it was having pushed Kubo too hard. He knew he had gone too far, but he had enjoyed it. He had persisted in trying to hurt Kubo out of pleasure at seeing his adversary hurt more deeply than himself. And he had let the feeling get out of control.

Asai had longed to wound his rival more deeply than he'd been wounded by him, but not to the point of smashing his skull open with a rock. Not to the point of leaving his blood-smeared face lying on the ground inside a triangle of three white stones. Psychological revenge would have been enough. If only Kubo had begged forgiveness...

Asai had been running along the prefectural highway for about twenty minutes, maybe. His knees were getting weak and his legs were wobbly. He still felt as if he were in one of those nightmares where he was trying to run but getting nowhere.

Then there were lights approaching from behind him, and he heard the noise of an engine. Asai began to tremble. They were already after him! The two bright round eyeballs got steadily bigger and more intense. The arrival of the pursuers felt exactly like the continuation of his nightmare. Had his dream world and reality become one and the same?

He gave up running and moved over to the side of the road, but didn't turn around. The headlights would illuminate his face and give his pursuers a clear look at him. Asai grabbed his dark glasses from his pocket and slipped them on. He had just enough sense left to think of that.

The car pulled up beside him. His heart felt as if it were going to explode. He heard the window roll down.

"Excuse me."

Asai froze.

"Are you headed to the station?" The man's tone was surprisingly amicable.

"Yep."

From behind his dark glasses, Asai could barely make out the speaker's face; then again, he wasn't really trying to look. He kept his head down.

"Great. That's on our way. Jump in!"

He realized there were two men in the car – the driver and someone in the passenger seat. He wondered if it was a trap. But there was no escape. Out here, there was nowhere to run to.

He climbed into the back seat and the car set off. Asai was seated behind the driver – a broad-shouldered man in a woollen jacket. The man in the passenger seat wore a leather jacket and was smoking a cigarette. His hair was long and quite messy, which gave him a feminine look. This reassured Asai a little – these men were obviously not police – but his heart rate only slowed very slightly.

The driver and the young man in the leather jacket resumed their conversation, but Asai couldn't hear what they were saying. His ears were ringing. Outside, the dark silhouettes of the mountains and fields flew past.

"What time's your train?"

The loud voice of the driver in the woollen jacket made Asai jump. The question had come out of nowhere. In fact, he had no idea. He'd never consulted the return train timetable. He'd been planning to spend the night either here in Fujimi or in neighbouring Kamisuwa, depending on how things went with Kubo.

"Hmm. At this time I'll take whichever train I can get," he replied.

"Back to Tokyo?"

"Yes."

Damn! He should have said he was going in the other direction. Now they knew he was from Tokyo. If he'd said he was headed the other way, once they'd dropped him off at the station they'd have had no way of knowing where he was going. But it was too late. If he changed his story now, it would seem bizarre. The younger man in the passenger seat looked at his watch, then said something in a low voice to the driver.

"It's 9.30 now. You'll have to wait for the eleven o'clock. It'll get you into Shinjuku at 4.30 in the morning."

Asai nodded in response.

"Were you visiting someone up at the sanatorium?"

The driver turned the wheel to the left. There was a sharp bend in the road, and then the sparse, distant lights of the town came into view.

"Yeah."

"It would help if the buses round here ran a bit later."

Asai caught sight of the driver's white gloves gripping the wheel, and almost cried out in horror. He must have left his fingerprints on the bottle of hair oil. He sat up. He was going to have to get them to stop the car and retrace his steps. He'd been right in the first place – he should have gone back to retrieve the bottle right away.

"So how's business up Tokyo way?"

"Huh?" Asai was thrown for a moment.

"We heard the economy's not too good right now. Us too – we're having a hard time of it with all these forced cuts in rice cultivation. I know the folks in the city think we have it good here in the country, they think we're making a fortune from farming, and until recently we were doing okay. But tonight we've just been to a meeting of the agricultural cooperative about the cuts and the new quotas, and it felt more like a funeral wake, I can tell you. Not long ago there was a union president who killed himself over these quotas."

These men were members of the local agricultural cooperative? He'd better be even more on his guard, Asai thought, sinking back again in his seat.

16

The Tokyo newspapers were filled with articles about the death of Konosuke Kubo. One paper ran with the headline "The Yatsugatake Mountain Murder Case". Another had "Fujimi Highlands Homicide". But the content was more or less the same.

At around 7 a.m. on Sunday morning, on a small rural road about a mile to the east of the prefectural highway in Fujimi, Nagano Prefecture, a local resident made the grisly discovery of a dead body. The man, estimated to be around forty, had been beaten to death with a rock. An examination of the contents of a suitcase found at the scene revealed that the murdered man was Konosuke Kubo, 38, of Keyaki Mansion, Higashi Nakano in Nakano Ward, Tokyo. Time of death was estimated to have been between 8 p.m. and 11 p.m. on Saturday evening.

The crime took place near the foot of the southern face of Mount Amigasa, one of the peaks in the Yatsugatake mountain ridge, near the upper ravine of the Kamanashi River. This is a remote area that is practically deserted after dark. By the victim's head lay three large, bloodstained stones, weighing approximately two kilos each. It is believed that these stones were used to deal fatal blows that fractured the victim's skull. Additionally, the face had been damaged by sulphuric acid, which strongly suggests that the killer first threw acid at the victim, then, once his target was on the ground, finished him off with the aforementioned stones. The particularly brutal method employed in this attack has led authorities to believe that the motive was likely to be some kind of personal grudge. There was no sign of a robbery.

Mr Kubo had arrived in the area on the evening train from Tokyo, with the intention of visiting his wife at a nearby sanatorium. He was attacked on his way from the station to the sanatorium. The killer left nothing behind him besides a small amount of acid in a 60ml bottle that had once contained hair oil. The bottle was old, and it is supposed that the killer refilled it with sulphuric acid and brought it to the site of the murder, making it probable that this was a premeditated act. A single fingerprint was lifted from the bottle, but it was reportedly too smudged to be of use in identifying the murderer. The bottle used was from a brand of hair oil popular among women and is widely available throughout the country, making it difficult to investigate its origin. From the use of the hair oil bottle, one theory is that the crime may have been committed by a woman.

Mr Kubo was the manager of the General Affairs department of his uncle's textiles firm in Kyobashi, Tokyo. According to his colleagues he was a rather quiet character, was not the type of person to make enemies, and had no history of affairs with women.

As previously stated, one theory of the crime is that of a grudge killing, but the fact that a hippy commune has recently taken up residence at the foot of the Yatsugatake ridge has also fuelled speculation that this could be a copycat killing, modelled on the infamous murder of the actress Sharon Tate by the fanatical followers of Charles Manson in the United States. Authorities are currently pursuing both leads.

On Monday morning, Asai purchased a selection of newspapers from the stand at the station and compared their versions of the story. They all contained more or less the same information.

He'd had a moment of panic when he read that there was a fingerprint discovered on the bottle of hair oil, but then calmed down when he saw that it was too indistinct to use as evidence. He knew that reporters tended to work with the police, so he believed it was true. He guessed that a fingerprint had to be clear to be of help in an investigation. If any part of it was smudged or too faint then it became unusable.

Asai was reminded of a famous case from a couple of years ago. Hundreds of millions of yen, being transported to a certain factory in the western suburbs of Tokyo for its workers' year-end bonuses, were stolen by thieves posing as traffic cops. The bank workers in charge of the transportation had voluntarily handed over the cash to the robbers, who'd turned up on the distinctive white motorbikes used by police, so the case did not legally qualify as an armed robbery. According to the newspaper, a partial fingerprint had been discovered on one of the duralumin cases that had contained the bags of bonus money. There had been hope that this might lead to the identification of the thieves, but all discussion of the fingerprint disappeared from the news the moment it was announced that a lump of red soil had also been discovered in the back of the van. The newspapers focused all their attention on the analysis of this piece of soil and the conclusion that it had come from a specific part of the Kanto region, but in the end it had led nowhere. When Asai had first read these reports, he'd found it hard to believe that someone who'd pulled off such a meticulously planned crime would have been careless enough to leave behind a lump of soil in the van. He guessed it had been left there deliberately in order to throw the detectives off the scent. When discussion of the lump of earth also disappeared from the news, Asai had been sure that the head of the investigation had realized he'd been taken in. Even grand-scale investigations in the public eye could fall prey to ruses like this. There was nothing that could be obtained from a blurry fingerprint on a bottle of hair oil. Asai felt pretty confident of this.

First and foremost, any fingerprint discovered in a criminal investigation would be compared to all the prints on file. But these files contained only the prints of former and current convicts, not the general public, so that search wouldn't turn up any useful result. And on top of that the fingerprint wasn't even clear.

Secondly, the hair oil bottle that had contained the acid was sold in vast quantities nationwide, so Asai agreed with the opinion expressed in the newspapers that this wouldn't turn out to be much of a clue. And it hadn't even been purchased recently. There was no chance of tracing a cosmetics bottle that his wife had bought over a year ago.

When he considered all these points, Asai was glad that he hadn't gone back to retrieve the bottle after all. He'd been worried about the possibility of his fingerprints being left on it, but now he realized it wasn't a big deal. If he'd persuaded himself to return to the scene of the crime, who knows what kind of bad luck he might have run into? The reports said that the body had been discovered around seven the next morning, which suggested that no one had passed by the spot until that time, but who might he have run into on the way there who could later have identified him to the police?

At that point, Asai realized that none of the newspapers had mentioned the two men from the agricultural cooperative – the men who had picked him up on the prefectural highway and dropped him off at Fujimi station. Surely, given the location and the lateness of the hour, they would have reported the encounter to the local police? It was strange that there was nothing written about them.

There were three possible explanations for this. Firstly, the police may have decided to keep this information secret for now. Another possibility was that the two men hadn't heard about the murder and therefore hadn't offered their evidence before the deadline for the articles going to press. In that case, it was likely that tomorrow's papers would carry the story of the suspect walking by the side of the prefectural highway who'd been given a lift to the local station. The third conceivable explanation was that the two men had not considered their story worth mentioning to the police as they didn't see any connection between the murder and the man they gave a lift to.

Asai had one more hypothesis – a rather over-optimistic one, perhaps, but one he couldn't ignore. He wondered if the two men had difficulty believing that a man who had just paid a visit to a loved one in the sanatorium could be walking calmly along the street towards the station moments after committing a brutal murder.

To Asai's surprise, there must have been some truth in this last theory, because neither the next day's newspapers, nor the following day's, nor all the days after that contained any mention of the man walking along the highway who had been picked up by a passing car. If the two men had reported the event to the police, then there was no reason why the press wouldn't have picked up on it and splashed it across their headlines. There was no point in keeping that kind of information under wraps. In fact, it would be useful to the investigation to have it out there, in the chance it might jog the memory of any other witnesses. Asai had to assume that the men didn't believe he could have had anything to do with the murder.

The early newspaper articles had focused repeatedly on the brutality of the murder, which apparently made it a grudge killing. At least that seemed to be what the investigators believed. But Asai's "brutality" hadn't been intentional. There hadn't been any plan. It had just happened, a product of circumstances, and he refused to admit any responsibility for it. If there was blame to be apportioned, then let it be the fault of momentum.

The newspapers still published claims, by people who knew him, that Konosuke Kubo wasn't the kind of person to have enemies; that there was no reason for anyone to murder him; that they rejected the theory of a revenge killing. Clearly nobody knew about the love affair with Eiko Asai that had so enraged her husband. Even Kubo himself had been unaware of Asai's anger. Asai had never spoken of his feelings to another soul.

However, there was one point that was worrying Asai – the detective agency that he had hired to investigate Konosuke Kubo. If the detective were to read in the newspaper that Kubo had been murdered, he could easily report his client to the police. But for now, there was nothing in the media on that subject.

Why not? Probably because private detective agencies respected their clients' privacy. If someone connected to one of their cases were killed, telling the police would go against their policy of complete confidentiality. Which should be their priority – professional confidentiality or the public good? (Offering information to a police investigation would fall here into the category of public good. Or perhaps you could say that complete respect of professional confidentiality was in fact *for* the public good.) It was a grey area, but as it looked as if the detective agency had revealed nothing to the police, Asai concluded that their professional reputation for absolute privacy was what they held sacred. This privacy must have been beneficial to both parties: the client requesting an investigation and the person investigated. The success of these agencies was founded on this principle of confidentiality, and because all parties were able to put their trust in this principle, business flourished.

Of course, Asai had added that extra layer of security, just in case, when he'd given the detectives a false name, address and place of work. They had never contacted him – he had always contacted them. His original request; the payment of an advance fee; his request for a second investigation; picking up of the report and settling of his account – he had done all these in person at the agency. He'd worn his dark glasses throughout, so that even if he were seen in the street, no one would recognize his face. If for some reason the detective decided to cooperate with the police, he wouldn't be able to give them Asai's name or where he came from. He was sure no one had imagined that he could be an employee of the Ministry of Agriculture and Forestry. It was precisely to avoid any possible trouble like this that Asai had settled on all these precautions before ever setting foot in the detective agency.

His final concern was Chiyoko Takahashi, but he guessed he didn't need to be too worried about her. Asai was certain she had no idea that he had found out the truth about his wife's death. She would never imagine that he knew of her relationship to Kubo, or that Eiko had died in his home. Hearing the news of Kubo's death, she would never connect it with Eiko or Eiko's family members. What was more, she herself had blackmailed the victim into giving up his house and the land it stood on, so her guilty conscience would stop her going to the police. She wouldn't want to draw any more attention to herself than necessary.

All in all, Asai felt fairly safe. He had carefully prepared for any eventuality, with the result that he had successfully created a zone of protection around himself. And yet he remained alert.

It was also fortunate for Asai that the media had run with the theory that Kubo's murder had been a nihilistic attack by members of the hippy commune at the base of the Yatsugatake ridge. A meaningless attack was the simplest and most fascinating explanation. The idea that a new American phenomenon had arrived in Japan – that following the current US-style recession, now even Japanese crimes were becoming Americanized – was a concept bound to thrill their readership.

It was the brutality of the crime that encouraged the press to make the connection with the hippy commune. Editorials and opinion pieces appeared, claiming that throwing acid in someone's face before smashing their skull with three separate stones – well, it was no ordinary killing; the motive could be a kind of social vengeance, just the same as the Manson Family, a cult that had killed in retaliation against modern society.

These articles must have created all kinds of problems for the poor Yatsugatake hippies. And yet, among all the opinion pieces on the subject, there was not a single one that suggested the killing might have been in self-defence.

The vision of Kubo's face, almost completely obscured by the darkness, surrounded by those three bloodied rocks, troubled Asai's conscience. Still, all he needed to do was put it out of his mind, and everything would be fine.

Every day at the ministry, Asai put everything he had into his job. He checked all kinds of texts and documents, adding his notes on a slip of paper for the attention of his superiors; met with manufacturers; attended meetings; drew up proposals. He was extremely busy as usual.

The killing on the Fujimi plateau began to fade in his memory. It had happened somewhere far away in place and time; his mind had already filed it in the "past events" section. He was completely detached from the reality of the experience. It wasn't anything he'd planned and engineered – it had been pure chance, and there was no objective involved in chance. And an action without objective is one with only a tenuous connection to reality.

Even so, Asai was not completely at peace. From time to time it would hit him that he was a murderer, a realization that made him break out in a sweat – not from any crisis of conscience, but out of the sheer terror of being found out. It resembled the fear of being pushed off a high cliff, and it sometimes made him want to shout out loud. It would strike him unexpectedly like an attack of stomach cramps. And then, just like stomach cramps, once the pain had passed he would forget it completely and return to his everyday life. He was never haunted by the ghost of Konosuke Kubo.

Things continued this way until mid-November.

One day in November, a representative from the Life Affairs Division of the Central Union of Agricultural Cooperatives turned up at the ministry. He brought with him a request for Asai to give a series of lectures on the food manufacturing industry.

"Where's it going to be?"

"The southern part of Nagano Prefecture. There's a farming village near Suwa that wants to put more emphasis on food manufacturing. They sent the request through the cooperative's Nagano branch. They specifically asked for the 'veteran Mr Asai'. There were some other lectures or workshops you gave before in other prefectures which were very well-received. It seems word has reached the people in Nagano, and they're insisting that the ministry send you."

Asai refused on the spot. Normally, with an assignment of this kind, he would ask for a couple of days to think it over, then politely turn down the offer.

"I've got a lot to do in the office at the moment. I really haven't got the time to go out to the countryside."

"That's fine. It doesn't have to be right away," the rep explained.

"I don't think I can get away for a while. It's not looking very promising."

There was absolutely no way that Asai could go to that part of Nagano Prefecture. What if he met the two men who had given him a lift in their car the night of the murder? The middle-aged man in the woollen jacket – the driver – was definitely on the board of the local agricultural cooperative. He'd mentioned they were on the way home from a meeting about the rice acreage reduction policy. He could well be one of the members who wanted to solve their farming community's financial problems by turning to the food manufacturing industry. If Asai went to Suwa, he might find himself face to face with the two men. He was sure they'd attend that sort of event. They might even be among the organizers.

That night on the road in Fujimi, he'd been wearing his dark glasses as a precaution, and it had been dark, so they probably hadn't got a good look at his face. But if they saw him again, it might reawaken some memory. And they'd had a short conversation while he was sitting in the back seat. They might well recognize his voice. And, even if they didn't recall his face, there could be some other physical characteristic of his that had left an impression in their minds. The safest move was to refuse. There was no need to put himself in a dangerous situation if it could be avoided.

"That's very disappointing. Is there really no way you can make it?"

"No, not this time." Asai knew he was being brusque.

"Please look at it from my point of view. Last time, you agreed to go to Yamanashi Prefecture, just next door. How am I going to explain to the Nagano members that you won't visit their prefecture? They're going to ask why you'll go to Yamanashi but not to Nagano."

It was true that he had given a series of lectures in Yamanashi at the start of autumn that year. Now he wished he hadn't. But that was before he'd smashed Konosuke Kubo's skull with three rocks at the foot of the Yatsugatake mountain ridge. Obviously, it hadn't been a premeditated act. If it had been, then he would never have gone to Yamanashi first.

He knew he needed to come up with an alternative.

"I'll find somebody to go in my place."

"They really want it to be you. They heard so much about the good advice you gave the people in Yamanashi. I'm here at the request of the Nagano prefectural cooperative, you know. Oh well, I guess I'll just have to give them the message."

"I'm sorry, but I just can't."

17

Asai checked the papers every day to see if there was any news about the case. He only had one newspaper delivered to his home, so he would check out the three other national dailies when he got to work.

For the next three weeks, there was nothing new on the subject, although there was plenty of coverage of new crimes. The papers seemed to be full of nothing else. It was as if there was no space available for any reporter who had decided to stick with a story – and perhaps none of them had the patience to see a story to its conclusion anyway. Clearly the editors believed that their readers needed a new story every day to hold their interest.

The Kubo case was now a thing of the past, thought Asai, or at least it was on its way to being. Like so many other murder cases, it would end up buried in some old file and forgotten.

Until now, he had been living in fear of the unseen investigation going on in Fujimi and had immersed himself in his work as a way to forget, but now he felt the pressure relax a little. He was able to get back to normal and breathe more freely. He felt the energy return to his body.

There was definitely no call to go visiting Nagano Prefecture at a time like this. Back on the highway in

Nagano he had made the smart decision not to go back to retrieve the hair-oil bottle, and it was the same deal now – it really wouldn't do to court danger by returning to the scene of the crime. He was glad that he'd turned down the cooperative's invitation. There were other people in the office perfectly capable of giving that lecture.

And then one day in the ministry cafeteria he happened to pick up a weekly news magazine that someone had left lying on a chair and began to flick through its pages. He glanced at a column entitled "News Follow-up", and his heart lurched in his chest.

The Yatsugatake Murder Mystery is widely rumoured to have been a cult killing committed by the local hippy commune, but recent information has come to light that has set the investigation task force looking in a different direction.

The body of Konosuke Kubo (38), manager of the General Affairs section at R-Textiles, located in Kyobashi, Chuo Ward, Tokyo, was discovered murdered on a country road on the Fujimi plateau in Nagano Prefecture, the morning of Sunday 26 October of this year. The crime appeared to have been committed some time the previous evening. The murderer first threw sulphuric acid in the victim's face then broke his skull with three separate rocks, in what was an exceedingly brutal killing. Mr Kubo met his tragic fate while on his way from Tokyo to visit his wife at the Fujimi Plateau Sanatorium. As nothing was stolen from the victim and it was believed that he had no enemies, the crime was dubbed a "gratuitous murder", and suspicion fell upon the hippy commune.

There was much talk of this being the Japanese version of the Charles Manson murders, but in subsequent investigations the police established that the hippies had nothing to do with the case. There had at one time been a considerable number of hippy communes in the Yatsugatake area, but, possibly because this lifestyle has recently fallen out of fashion, most of them moved away around the autumn and in fact hardly any hippies remain.

The latest information obtained by the task force was that around 9.30 p.m. on the evening of 25 October, a lone man was seen walking on the prefectural highway in the vicinity of the sanatorium by two members of the local agricultural cooperative, Mr Akiharu Kido (40) and Mr Jiro Haruta (23). It seems that Mr Kido and Mr Haruta gave the man a lift, dropping him off in front of Fujimi station. The man in question appeared to be around forty years old, but as it was dark and he was wearing tinted glasses, the two witnesses didn't get a good look at him. In the course of a conversation that took place in the car, the man claimed to have visited the sanatorium. However, according to police inquiries, no visitors left the sanatorium around that hour. The part of the highway where the man was picked up was very near to the junction with the country road on which the victim was discovered, and the police are currently investigating whether this event could have any connection with the crime.

In the car, the man said he was taking the train back to Tokyo that evening. The victim, Mr Kubo, was also from Tokyo, so it is possible that the man was an acquaintance of his who had travelled with him to Fujimi, and that he was Mr Kubo's killer. Thus the "gratuitous murder" might well turn out to be a grudge killing after all, and the task force is now thoroughly reinvestigating all of Mr Kubo's professional and personal relationships.

Recently, the press had stopped bothering to publish follow-up reports in the dailies, leaving the weekly news magazines to publish longer articles that covered such cases in more detail. Asai looked at the date on the front page. It was already a week old. He never usually bothered reading this kind of magazine, so this was the first he'd heard of any new developments.

All of his fears came rushing back. Of course; the two men who'd picked him up from the highway had reported it to the police after all. That secure feeling of distance between the killing and himself was gone. It was back before his eyes, in lurid colour.

Leaving his lunch untouched on the table, he gulped down a full glass of water. He had to compose himself, to consider the content of this article calmly. He had to work out whether the information it contained meant he was in imminent danger.

The two men had said that they couldn't clearly see the face of the forty-year-old man because he was wearing dark glasses. That was exactly what he'd supposed, so wearing the glasses had worked. The article hadn't mentioned it, but one reason they hadn't been able to see his face properly was that he'd been deliberately looking down at the floor the whole time. He had engineered it so they couldn't see his face. He wasn't surprised that they hadn't any particular impression of his features, and he was sure there wouldn't be enough for the police to put together an identikit.

It also said in the article that the suspect had told them he was taking the Tokyo train from Fujimi station. To be precise, it was the driver of the vehicle who had mentioned it, assuming that Asai was travelling back to Tokyo. Asai had done nothing but murmur in agreement, and then the older man – Akiharu Kido, member of the agricultural cooperative, according to the magazine – had begun discussing Tokyo train times with the younger Jiro Haruta.

At the time Asai had regretted not telling them he was taking a train in the opposite direction. He'd even been on the point of changing his story, but had decided that being from Tokyo wasn't enough to be identified. The article mentioned that the police believed the suspect was an acquaintance of Konosuke Kubo's from Tokyo, and that they were re-interviewing everyone who knew him. Thanks to the business with the train, Asai had briefly worried that he was in danger. However, he was sure that no matter who the police questioned about Kubo's connections, his name would never come up. No one knew about him. They were going to end up in the same place as before, unable to discover any motive for the murder.

In conclusion: no, he wasn't in any immediate danger after all. At first glance, the article had chilled him to the bone, but now he realized it was nothing. He felt calm again.

Three or four days later, the delegate from the Central Union of Agricultural Cooperatives came to visit Asai once more.

"Mr Asai, I let the Nagano Prefectural branch know that you couldn't make it. Yesterday they got back to me and said they were dead set on it being you who gives the lectures. Is there any way you can make it work?"

Asai gave the delegate a stern look.

"Didn't you manage to find anyone to go in my place?"

"No. I tried to negotiate it with the Nagano people, but they didn't want anyone else." The rep simpered a little. "They said it absolutely had to be you."

"Tell them that I have things to do; I can't just re-arrange my schedule to suit everyone. Please tell them 'no'."

"You're sure there's no way...?"

"Absolutely sure. There are plenty of other people at my level who are just as capable of delivering lectures."

"Well, actually, there aren't. We've looked into it, and you're really the only one, Mr Asai. The Nagano coopera-tive believes you're the ideal candidate."

"Now come on, I don't need you to pressure me too! I told you, I can't."

"I'm in a bit of a fix here. Your advice was so well-received in Yamanashi. If you could just pop over to their neighbours and give them a helping hand too —"

"I'm really busy here at the ministry. I can't go on any business trips right now, and that's the end of it," said Asai. His tone was harsh.

"So when do you think you'll be able to get away?"

Asai struggled to come up with a response.

"I mean, when do you think things will be a little less busy at work?"

"I couldn't tell you. I just can't go. Turn them down, please." Asai waved his hand frantically in front of his face in an unmistakable gesture of refusal.

It was out of the question for him to go to southern Nagano Prefecture. In fact, not only the south; the whole of the prefecture could be risky. If the lectures were organized by the prefectural branch of the cooperative, then members from anywhere in the region were free to attend.

Akiharu Kido and Jiro Haruta... He had to memorize those names. Especially Kido – he was the older man and likely to be an influential figure in the Fujimi branch. He could show up anywhere, anytime. Asai was going to have to be vigilant.

For the next ten days, there was nothing in particular to worry Asai. The delegate from the Central Union didn't show his face again. As there was no more talk of finding a replacement for him, Asai assumed that the union had sent some sort of technical expert from the agricultural experiment station. It made more sense than sending a bureaucrat like himself. Technology ought to be the domain of the experts.

And then a letter arrived from Kobe, from the president of Yagishita Ham. The first part of the letter laid out the problems facing farmers in Tottori Prefecture. It continued:

> There, as elsewhere in the country, interest is moving away from the cultivation of rice, and towards the modern food-manufacturing industry. There are plans under way for a week-long conference on these techniques, sponsored by the union of agricultural cooperatives. They're

hoping to invite some professors from agricultural universities in Tokyo as speakers, along with engineers from some of the biggest companies in the business. They've also asked me if I could get you to come along for just a couple of days. I guess it's because they've heard that you and I are on good terms.

The vice-chairman of the prefectural branch and I have been friends for a while. He's a very good type. He says that your attendance, Mr Asai, as assistant division chief at the Ministry of Agriculture, would lend his conference prestige and encourage more people to attend. He's hoping to have a chance to show you around while you're there. He'd like to take you to Daisen-Oki National Park and the Tottori sand dunes, as well as the famous radium hot springs at Misaki. I know that you're busy, so I hope that this request is not too troublesome...

Yagishita added that he really hoped Asai could fulfil the vice-chairman's request.

The approach came from his old friend Yagishita, and Asai didn't want to put him in an awkward position. He'd never been to Tottori Prefecture, and the thought of being shown around the famous tourist spots was very appealing. To be honest, he wasn't all that busy at work right now.

But there was a problem. If he accepted the trip to Tottori, then the Nagano people would be on to him again. Asai couldn't justify going to Tottori after turning down Nagano. He'd already been asked why he'd been willing to visit Yamanashi but not the neighbouring Nagano. If he were to go all the way to Tottori now, which was much further afield, there would be huge protests from the Nagano agricultural cooperative.

Yagishita had written that the attendance of the ministry's assistant division chief would add prestige to the conference. So that was it; that was why Nagano Prefecture was also insisting so strongly that he attend their events.

It was flattering to realize that people thought of him that way, but right now it was a compliment Asai could have done without. He realized that although people in rural areas might complain a lot about political interference, they still had a lot of respect for central government authority.

Yagishita called him on the phone.

"I got your reply to my letter," he began in his trademark gravelly voice. "I understand that you're very busy at the moment, but the Tottori people are desperate to have you come. Is there nothing you can do?"

"I'm sorry," Asai replied curtly. He knew that Yagishita could be very persistent, so he made his reply as unambiguous as possible.

"It's not for quite a while yet."

"It's still not going to be possible. The end of the year's coming up, and I just can't make any trips out of the city right now."

"That's quite a problem."

"I'm sorry to cause you trouble, but it can't be helped. If some of the professors from Tokyo attend, won't that be enough?"

"Seems that's not going to satisfy them. The Tottori people have heard so many good things about Mr Asai from the Ministry of Agriculture."

"You can tell me that all you like, but nothing's going to change my mind."

"There's nothing I can do?"

"Nothing."

"You don't seem to be in the best of moods today. I'll call back another time."

"You can call me as many times as you want, but the answer will still be no. It's got nothing to do with my mood. Please tell the people in Tottori it's no use asking."

"All right, all right. Anyhow... I've got a few things to do in Tokyo, so —"

"You're welcome to come to Tokyo if you want, but I have to ask you not to talk to me any more about this business."

"Right then. Speak to you soon." Yagishita laughed and hung up.

A determined man like Yagishita doesn't cave that easily, thought Asai. It was to be expected that he would follow up the letter with a phone call. He'd probably already promised the vice-chairman of the prefectural cooperative that Asai would be there. It'd be just like Yagishita to have told the man that he and Assistant Division Chief Asai were as thick as thieves. He'd doubtless assured him that it'd be no problem to convince Asai to come. In fact, his attendance would already be guaranteed. Well, we'll see who ends up going, thought Asai. He wasn't being deliberately awkward; it was just for his own safety.

Four days later, Yagishita called again.

"So can I count on you?"

"No."

"There's still time. Think it over some more."

"There's nothing to think over. I'm up to my neck in end-of-year stuff. There's no way I can make it."

"Can't you find a way?"

Asai hung up the phone. Although he was used to Yagishita's stubbornness, Asai felt that this time he was being obnoxious. But in fact neither Yagishita nor Tottori were being obnoxious. It was that Nagano Prefecture had approached him first. If only they hadn't, he could have been enjoying a soak in a hot spring this December.

Had Nagano Prefecture finally given up, though? He hadn't heard anything from them recently.

Three days later, Asai was waiting in front of the lifts to go down to the ground floor when one arrived from below and its door opened. The chief cabinet secretary stepped out, accompanied by Director-General Shiraishi. The chief cabinet secretary was slim and graceful like a crane, Director-General Shiraishi thick and clumsy as a bear. Asai bowed to them both.

The two men set off along the corridor, but after just a few steps Shiraishi abruptly turned and started back towards Asai. From the faintly magnanimous smile pasted on his face, Asai knew that he had some favour to ask of him. The heavy figure came ambling towards him, and Asai reacted by stepping a couple of paces towards his boss.

"How are you? Doing better?"

The director general spoke gently. He was clearly asking Asai how things had gone since Eiko had passed away. It was the right kind of concern for a supervisor to a member of his staff, but with a little hint of condescension thrown in.

"I'm fine, thank you," Asai replied with a bow.

"Glad to hear it. By the way, I've had a request from the Nagano Prefectural Cooperative to go and observe their operations, so I'm planning to spend around three days there from the middle of next week. They're claiming it's about all the recent changes in government policy, but really they're just looking for an excuse to lobby for their own case. Well, now it's impossible to ignore them. Agricultural produce, beef, pork, all those kinds of food processing – these are going to be the mainstays from here on. I want to take you with me, so could you start working on that, please? We haven't been on a business trip together since that time in Kobe, have we?"

Asai was speechless.

"Yes; back then it really was too bad what happened to your wife. Let's hope this trip will be more of a pleasant experience."

Still, he failed to come up with a response.

"Are you all right with that?"

"Yes", Asai finally managed to mumble.

The director general rejoined the chief cabinet secretary. Asai watched as the two men, walking side by side, disappeared around the next corner. Minutes later he was still there, staring into the distance, his mind completely blank.

The next lift arrived and opened its doors. But since no one got on, it simply closed them again and continued its lonely descent.

18

When Director-General Shiraishi left for Nagano, Asai wasn't with him. Two days earlier he had officially applied for sick leave because of a cold with a high fever.

How could he go to Nagano, knowing he was putting himself in such a dangerous situation?

Asai knew that it would be damaging to his reputation at the ministry, but he could see no other way out. He counted on finding some way to make it up to the director general later.

Like a pampered child, Shiraishi was unpredictable, tending to sudden mood swings. It would be fair to call him temperamental. An office veteran like Asai knew that his boss wouldn't stay angry with him for long. A decent manager would be aware of what a loss it would be if a knowledgeable and able subordinate like Asai turned his back on him. Moreover, Shiraishi was hardly devoted to his current post; his eye was already on the office of Director-General of Agricultural Affairs or even Director-General of Agriculture. He had no time to make a fuss about petty matters.

When that day in front of the lifts Shiraishi had suddenly asked Asai to accompany him to Nagano, Asai's gut instinct had been to accept on the spot. That had caused all kinds of problems later. His inability to refuse showed how much the director general intimidated him. It didn't matter how much of a spoilt child someone was; when they held that post they were different, special. A man like Asai, who had spent years working his way up through the ministry, had never lost that deferential attitude.

For about four or five days after agreeing to go to Nagano, he had felt depressed. Soon afterwards, his division chief had officially informed Asai that he would be accompanying Shiraishi on the field trip. As the request had come from the director general personally, there was no way to refuse. The sick leave had been his last resort. He had barely managed to avoid the danger.

Asai would probably have been all right in Nagano, but you never knew. Potentially, he could have run into the two men who'd given him a lift that night, and although the magazine article said they didn't remember his face, seeing him again might conceivably have jogged their memory. He really didn't feel like participating in a game of Russian roulette.

One of the junior managers in the division had been scrambled to replace him at the last moment. He reported back to Asai that his absence had been deeply regretted.

"They told me that they were determined to get you to come the next time. In fact, they're already planning their next event. They say they're not interested in inviting a bunch of high-level names. They want to hold a special training course and invite people with practical know-how like you to run it for them."

Obviously that was out of the question. If he was going to keep himself safe, it would be a while before he was able to accept invitations from anywhere in Japan.

He hadn't seen Director-General Shiraishi since then. He knew that he ought to apologize for the inconvenience that his feigned illness had caused, but he couldn't bring himself to visit the director general's office in person. When he made his reappearance at work following his supposed recovery, he went only to the division chief to express his regret. His manager didn't seem particularly bothered.

"You were ill. It couldn't be helped. I'll mention it to the director general."

Asai felt quite offended. At that moment he realized how easily he could be replaced by any number of different people. This division chief was also a career-track bureaucrat, and, just like Shiraishi, Asai knew he didn't plan to be in the post for long. His type was far less interested in the content of the job than in being careful not to rock the boat.

Asai assumed that Shiraishi would communicate his displeasure via a message sent through the division chief, but this wasn't the case. Despite the director general having asked Asai personally to accompany him to Nagano, it turned out that he didn't specifically want him at all – it could have been anybody. Asai supposed that when his replacement had reported how disappointed the locals had been by his absence, it was probably just flattery after all. They might well intend to invite him again sometime, but they weren't all that bothered. Or perhaps he was just overthinking it.

Asai knew he should take care not to become too obsessed by the Kubo case. Of course, he needed to be cautious, but he shouldn't get neurotic about it. It was important to stay calm.

For the moment, there was nothing too worrying. There'd been no more articles on the murder in the newspapers or the weekly magazines, nor any sign that the investigation was closing in on any one suspect. Crimes committed in idyllic, pastoral locations such as the Yatsugatake ridge or the Fujimi plateau, no matter how fascinating to the reader, always had to yield to sordid tales from the big city. There must have been no progress in the investigation, so nothing new to report.

He told himself that he'd pay a visit to Director-General Shiraishi as soon as he could and apologize in person for his absence, but somehow time got away from him. The year came to an end and the new one began. The director general gathered his whole staff for an opening-of-year speech, but Asai was hardly going to stand up in front of everyone and start offering excuses.

Throughout January and February, he never once had the opportunity to be alone with Shiraishi. Asai often saw him at a distance, but the director general was always surrounded by people. There were no more chance meetings in front of the lifts. That was the thing about fate – sometimes the opportunities came thick and fast, and then suddenly there'd be none whatsoever.

And then finally, at the beginning of March, he ran into Shiraishi in the foyer of the ministry. The director general was apparently on his way out to lunch alone. Asai stopped him as he sauntered towards the door where his car was waiting.

Three months had already passed, which made it rather late for Asai to be making his excuses, but it had been weighing on his mind and he had to get it out.

"Sir," he began, bowing low as he approached. "Last year... in December, I'm terribly sorry that I wasn't able to accompany you."

The director general stopped in his tracks. He turned his heavy frame slowly to face Asai, and the expression in his eyes in that moment revealed he had no idea what the other man was talking about. Asai continued.

"Er... When you went on that business trip to Nagano last year, I caught a bad cold at the last minute, and wasn't able to accompany you."

He bowed once more.

"Ah." The vague stare in Shiraishi's eyes finally seemed to give way to comprehension.

"Ah yes, I see. That time... Hmm. So, are you feeling better?" Shiraishi was speaking, but there was no thought behind it, and as the words hung empty in the air he was already moving again towards his waiting car.

"Yes, thank you, sir. I'm fine." He'd hardly still be suffering from a cold caught three months previously!

"Take care of yourself."

"Thank you, sir."

As he watched the clumsy figure of his boss walking away, Asai immediately regretted having brought up the subject. Director-General Shiraishi hadn't even given a second thought to Asai's cancellation.

He hadn't much cared who it was who came with him. All he'd cared about was having someone in his entourage. Those words he'd said to Asai in front of the lifts had been no more than an attempt to seem amiable.

Directors high up in the hierarchy often came out with stuff like that. They were trying to make themselves popular with their employees. It was just hot air – there was no heart involved.

There had been nothing to fret about. Asai wasn't even part of Shiraishi's consciousness – to the extent that he had even forgotten that his junior had been supposed to accompany him to Nagano. Asai was both disappointed that he'd made all that fuss for nothing, and at the same time it brought him some relief. His sadness was that of the petty functionary who was always too concerned about the opinions of his superiors. Even though he thought Shiraishi a mediocre man, Asai had suffered from the oppression of the system for years and didn't know how to change. He envied the younger employees – they seemed more able to speak their own minds.

But then it was a good thing that the director general wasn't concerned about him; it meant there was no danger of being forced to go to Nagano. Rather than feeling depressed over his own subservient attitude towards his bosses, Asai ought to be celebrating.

For a while, everything carried on as normal. The weather was unstable, fluctuating between cold and milder temperatures, then finally settled down and it began to feel like spring.

The newspapers featured new murder cases daily. The killers were always caught right away. Even if they escaped, they would eventually be found to have committed suicide. In every case, the identity of the killer was always discovered through his or her relationship with the victim. There was always some third party connected with the case who could shed light on its motive and its causes. Without this information, the police would have been at a loss.

All kinds of books of codes and regulations were lined up across Asai's desk, all necessary for his work as an administrator, among them of course the *Roppo Zensho*, the compendium of Japanese laws. Chapter 25, entitled "Corruption", pertained to civil servants.

Article #197: If a public official or a third party intermediary is found to have accepted a bribe or demanded a bribe, or entered into an agreement to offer or accept a bribe, he shall receive a sentence of no more than three years. If he is found to have accepted a solicitation, he shall receive a sentence of no more than five years.

Strangely enough, the section regarding homicide appeared right after the chapter on corruption of public officials.

Chapter 26: Homicide
Article #199: Persons guilty of committing murder shall be either put to death or imprisoned for a term of between three years and life.

The fact that homicide closely succeeded corruption seemed to imply that public officials were likely to commit murder.

The Criminal Procedure Code

Article #250: The statute of limitations applies as follows:
1) 15 years for crimes punishable by death
2) 10 years for crimes punishable by imprisonment for life, or life with hard labour

3) 7 years for crimes punishable with a sentence of more than 10 years' imprisonment or hard labour.

Seven to fifteen years. Asai considered this period of time. The scale he used was the number of years of public service he had left. Fifteen years would take him to one year after retirement age. In ten he would probably already be division chief. Seven would be right around the time that his promotion was being considered.

The whole incident in Fujimi was fading from his consciousness, but from time to time he would start making these calculations. It wasn't out of fear of being arrested. He wanted to know how soon the statute of limitations would be up so that he'd be able to live a completely carefree existence.

He was in the middle of one of these moments of reflection when the president of Yagishita Ham arrived on a trip from Kobe.

"So what brings you to Tokyo?" Asai asked. He'd taken Yagishita to a nearby café. It was lunchtime, and men and women from the various government ministries were out strolling in the park.

"A thank-you gift for all our franchise stores. We're taking them to a spa in Hokkaido."

"Wow. You're always up to something."

"There's a lot of competition these days. Our firm only offers domestic travel tickets, but there are other companies who organize group tours overseas."

"Which ones?"

"Kurosaki, the agricultural equipment manufacturers, for example. Well, machinery makers are a whole different ball game – their sales are on a different level to ours. We can't make the same kind of offers to the sausage and ham vendors. I've heard that at the end of March they're organizing a courtesy trip to Southeast Asia for the executive members of all the agricultural cooperatives in the Koshinetsu region."

"The whole of Koshinetsu? That's going to be quite a number."

"Seems they've kept it to about forty people – the people with the most influence in the region, I imagine. This time it's not the prefectural-level executives they're taking, but local members from the towns and villages. The managing director at Kurosaki Machinery is a friend of mine, so I heard it from him. This rice acreage reduction policy – well, it's got everyone in the agricultural equipment business quite worried. They've carefully hand-picked the local members over the big guns. They've decided they need to turn their attentions to the regional level."

"Everyone's feeling the pinch, eh?"

"Yep, tough times for tradesmen too."

A couple of days later, the division director summoned Asai.

"Asai, the Nagano Prefectural co-op is sponsoring a short seminar. Can you attend?"

Startled, he repeated what he thought he'd heard. "Nagano Prefecture?"

"Yep. There's been a joint request from both the national and prefectural unions for a series of lectures to be held in the region."

Asai felt irritated. Nagano again – seriously? Why were they being so stubborn?

"Whereabouts in Nagano?"

"The south. They want you to give a lecture in each of the southern regions over a period of five days. By the way, I got this request directly from Director-General Shiraishi's office."

"From the director general?"

"That's right. He feels strongly that with the new agricultural policies the ministry should offer as much support to the farmers at the local level as possible. I know it's a lot of trouble for you, but we'd like you to be the one to go, seeing as you are so familiar with the politics and administration of food processing."

"Did they ask for me... um... I mean did the Nagano people request me specifically?"

"Not exactly. Well, they said they wanted someone with experience, and Mr Shiraishi told me to send you."

"The director general wanted me?"

"It seems you made a specific request to be dispatched. He says you told him how disappointed you were when you got ill and were unable to accompany him to Nagano back in December last year, and that you'd told him you definitely wanted to go the next time."

"Ah, yes. Well, that... er..."

He hadn't spoken to Shiraishi because he wanted to be sent to Nagano. He'd only meant to apologize for cancelling the first time. Shiraishi had misunderstood his motive. But Asai could hardly tell that to his division chief.

"The director general clearly remembered your request. The tour will be for five days, starting 1 April. I expect you'll get the formal request shortly."

"Which districts of southern Nagano exactly?"

"Ina, Takato, Iida, Fujimi and Chino. It'll be five nights and six days."

There was no way for Asai to refuse, not after last time, and now he was being recommended personally by the director general.

Faking a sudden illness wasn't going to work this time, either. He couldn't play that card twice.

His mistake had been to approach Shiraishi in the first place. The director general had long since forgotten that Asai had pulled out of the December tour, because it hadn't been an issue for him. He'd had a bad feeling at the time that his apology was unnecessary, and he turned out to have been right. He should have let sleeping dogs lie.

A five-night, six-day tour of a relatively small area meant he was practically guaranteed to meet Akiharu Kido and Jiro Haruta. The lectures would be attended exclusively by members of the agricultural cooperative. And it wouldn't only be lectures – there would be receptions, dinner parties, and other get-togethers in the evenings. All the local members would look forward to attending these events, and he was sure to run into the two men there too. Asai would be seated in the place of honour, and each attendee would come in turn to drink a toast. Mr Kido and Mr Haruta would be right there in front of him. Country types could down a lot of alcohol, and their parties went on late. There'd be plenty of time for the men to remember him.

If only I'd never met those two, thought Asai. He'd have been fine if there was no chance of Kido and Haruta turning up. He knew that he'd keep imagining their eyes on him, even while giving a lecture. He'd never be able to completely relax, have to be constantly on his guard.

Why did he keep being reeled back in to a place that he was desperately trying to avoid? He felt as if he were slowly going crazy.

And then he remembered his recent conversation with Yagishita.

Kurosaki Machinery was inviting members of the agricultural cooperatives in the Koshinetsu area on a tour of Southeast Asia beginning at the end of March. Nagano was part of the Koshinetsu area. The participants were being selected from small local cooperatives according to this policy of "hand-picking".

What if Kido and Haruta were on the list of attendees? The end of March was around the time of the lecture tour. There was still a chance he might be able to avoid bumping into them.

There was a glimmer of hope in Asai's heart. He needed to get hold of a copy of Kurosaki Machinery's list of attendees as soon as possible. If the tour was to begin at the end of March, it should already be drawn up.

Asai waited impatiently for Yagishita to get back from his Hokkaido spa retreat.

19

Yagishita stopped by in Tokyo on his way back from Hokkaido, and called Asai at the ministry. Asai had left him a message at Yagishita Ham's Tokyo branch office.

"I'm back," he said, coughing. "It was freezing up there; I caught a cold. Anyway, they told me you phoned."

His voice was more gravelly than ever.

"It's nothing important, but I'd really like to meet you for dinner tonight if you're free. How about it?"

"I don't see why not. Shall I bring along someone from our office?"

"No, no. Just the two of us. I've got a bit of a favour I want to ask you."

"Okay. Got it."

Normally it was Yagishita who played the host, but this time Asai had invited the other man to join him, so Asai made all the arrangements.

They met in a café in Shinjuku at six that evening. Yagishita was coughing and constantly wiping his nose.

"There was still snow on the ground in Hokkaido. We went to the hot springs in Noboribetsu. The water was hot, of course, but I still caught a chill when I got out."

"Why did you choose Hokkaido at this time of year?"

"Everyone's been to Shirahama or Atami these days.

Despite the weather, I thought it would be better to travel a little further afield. My guests were all impressed that they could sit in the open-air baths in the snow, but it was way colder than I'd imagined. Still, the inns were really quiet, and the service was great."

So Yagishita had picked Hokkaido because Shirahama or Atami weren't luxurious enough for his guests, but he'd deliberately gone in the off season to save money on the accommodation. Asai recalled his earlier complaint that he couldn't afford to offer expensive freebies to his sausage and ham vendors, especially when compared with Kurosaki Machinery's tour of Southeast Asia.

He couldn't ask for a favour over a single cup of coffee, so Asai took his guest to a nearby restaurant that specialized in the cuisine of Northeast Japan. It was a simple place; the type with stools instead of chairs. The counter was completely empty, but Asai chose the table in the far corner. They ordered sake and a regional speciality, a *Shottsuru*-style hotpot made with salted, fermented fish. This simple fare was all the rules allowed a public employee to treat a visiting businessman to, but the hot broth turned out to be just the thing for Yagishita with his cold.

As they drank and chatted, Asai wondered when the best moment would be to broach the topic. He couldn't bring it up right away. He'd thought over what to say, but the content was very different from the usual stuff he talked about with Yagishita, so he was very conscious that he'd have to be careful with his wording to avoid arousing the other man's suspicions.

About an hour passed. Yagishita also seemed to be preoccupied with whatever this "bit of a favour" was that

Asai wanted from him. It would be best not to wait too long; it'd be more difficult to talk when the restaurant filled up with customers.

"So, Mr Yagishita, you mentioned the other day that you were on good terms with the managing director of Kurosaki Machinery."

Asai took care to make the question sound like the natural progression of their conversation. Yagishita nodded and put down his sake cup.

"Yes, that's right. I know him. In fact, he's a friend of mine. He's the younger brother of the president's wife, and a shrewd businessman."

"I have something I need to ask him, but it's a bit delicate, and I wonder if you could do it for me?"

"What kind of thing?"

"Well, you see, it's a request that was passed to me by someone else – someone I'm connected to at work. It's not something I can refuse, unfortunately. You can see what kind of a position I'm in?"

He left his friend to imagine for a moment.

"Yes, I get it," said Yagishita, with a nod. "You're an old hand at this, so everyone is asking you to do stuff for them. It must be coming at you from all sides."

He clearly had in mind one of Asai's bosses or someone very prominent in the business world.

"Yes, that's pretty much it. But it's hard being an old hand when you're still just a petty functionary."

"No, that's not what I'm saying," said Yagishita hurriedly, conscious that he might have committed a faux pas. "I'm talking about how you've been an influential power for quite a while now. Don't take it the wrong way."

"Never mind about all that," replied Asai good-humouredly. He poured Yagishita another cupful of sake. "Anyway, we all have our obligations."

"I understand. Thank you. Anyway, what is it I can ask Yada about for you? Yada – that's Kurosaki's managing director."

"Right, well… This is the situation. For various reasons, I can't reveal the name of the person who passed on this request to me. Anyway, this is what it's about. Do you remember when you told me how Kurosaki Machinery had invited some of the influential names in the cooperative to go on a tour of Southeast Asia at the end of March? I suppose the participants have already been chosen?"

"Yes, they must have been if they're going that soon. It's overseas travel, so there are passports and things that need to be prepared."

"Yes, I suppose there are."

"So what about it?"

Asai took a deep breath. "Well, the person in question wants to know whether the names Akiharu Kido and Jiro Haruta from Nagano are on the list of participants or not."

"I can't tell you that off the top of my head, but I can ask Yada. He'll tell me right away. If you like, I can call him right now." Yagishita straightened up and checked his watch. "Oh no – sorry. It's too late. He'll have gone home by now."

"Don't worry. It's not that urgent."

"Really? All right then. Will tomorrow be okay?"

"Tomorrow's fine. But I'm sorry to say I've one more request. This one isn't quite so easy."

"What is it?"

Asai needed a moment to summon his courage. He took a long sip from his sake cup.

"Right, well, it's very annoying to have been asked this, but I may as well just come out with it. If Kido and Haruta aren't already on the list, is there any way you can get Kurosaki to add them to it?"

"Add them?" Yagishita coughed in surprise. He looked very reluctant, but Asai had been prepared for this.

"Of course, that person – I mean the man who asked me this favour – is prepared to pay the full cost of travel for these two individuals," he explained hurriedly. "He doesn't want to inconvenience Kurosaki Machinery, but he would be very grateful if they could be included in the group tour."

"If he pays the costs himself, then it might be possible," Yagishita conceded. "But what the heck is all this about? I mean, what is this person thinking?"

"Yes, obviously I asked him the same thing, and it appears to be as simple as wanting them to enjoy an overseas trip. There may be some sort of obligation involved, but I really don't know much about it. Individual travel is rather expensive, but it only costs about half the amount to join a tour group. He must have realized that."

"Yes, I see. To save on costs the best thing is to get them on a tour. I get that." Yagishita's roots as a Kansai business-man meant that economy was something he understood very well.

"Kurosaki Machinery's tour is going to be six nights and seven days and take in Hong Kong, Macau and Taiwan."

Asai had got this information by calling the headquarters of the National Union of Agricultural Cooperatives and using a false name. The tour would leave Haneda Airport on 31 March and return the night of 6 April. The two men wouldn't get back to Nagano until the seventh, after Asai's lecture tour would have finished.

"About the expenses: I believe it'll come to around 170,000 or 180,000 yen per person – 350,000 or 360,000 for the two of them. If the plan gets the go-ahead from Kurosaki Machinery, I've been authorized to hand over the cash in full right away."

"Hey, hey – just a minute. I can't tell you anything until I've had the chance to talk to Mr Yada."

"Of course not."

"And if this Mr Kido and Mr Haruta are already on the list then we don't need to worry about all this, do we?"

"Sure."

Asai thought how perfect it would be if they did happen to be on the tour: 350,000 or 360,000 yen was quite a sum of money. But he was willing to pay it in order to save his own life. He'd backed himself into such a corner that he was willing to dig into his savings and come up with close to 400,000 yen. On the other hand, if the two men were already participating in the tour, he'd get away without paying a penny. When he put it like that, coughing up so much money was a totally crazy thing to do. It was a ridiculously convoluted scheme just to get these two men out of the way for the week of his lecture series.

"But one thing, Mr Asai. Kurosaki Machinery went through a very strict selection process among the Koshinetsu region cooperatives in order to pick the participants. The people they chose in the end must be some pretty big names."

Asai considered this point. Neither of the men who'd given him a lift had looked like they'd be influential in the politics of farming. The younger one in particular, this Jiro Haruta, wouldn't be on the list of invitees. Asai knew he was going to have to pay up. If he was lucky, Akiharu Kido might be on the list, and then it'd only cost him half.

Back then, what on earth had possessed him to get into their car? If he'd just refused, he wouldn't be in this predicament now. More to the point, why did that damned car have to be travelling on that particular stretch of road at that time in the evening?

Asai surprised himself by squeezing his sake cup so hard that it almost shattered in his grip. He felt very agitated all of a sudden.

Yagishita promised to visit Kurosaki Machinery's Tokyo headquarters the next day to find out whether the two men were signed up for the tour. If they weren't, he promised to find some pretext to get them added to the list by the managing director.

"Thank you for understanding. I hope I can count on you to be discreet. It's vital that no one knows the request came from me, otherwise I'll be put in a very awkward position at work. If anyone goes digging around, it could cause all kinds of trouble for the person in question. I know it might sound like I'm exaggerating, but I really need you to keep it all hush-hush."

Yagishita coughed again, and patted Asai reassuringly on the shoulder.

"Consider it done. I know you're in a difficult position. I'm already in your debt, and I know I'll need your support in the future too. You have my word – I won't tell a soul it was you. You can count on me – Yada's my friend, and he'll understand the situation."

Asai was a little disturbed to see that Yagishita was rather drunk already.

Yagishita called the following afternoon.

"Mr Asai, what we talked about last night... I went to see my friend and it turns out neither of the two people we discussed were on the list."

His voice sounded nasal. Apparently his cold hadn't got any better.

"I thought that might be the case."

Asai was very conscious of his colleagues sitting nearby, but he still couldn't completely hide his shock. It was like a sword to his heart. He had been hoping for better news. Now he had to compose himself and wait for the response to his next request. It didn't matter whether this would cost him 400,000 or even 500,000 yen. He didn't need to borrow it; he had the money there in his account. It was almost as if he had saved up in expectation of this very eventuality. He felt the heat rise in his body; his back was burning. He needed to hear the result of Yagishita's negotiations as soon as possible.

"Are you ready? I'm just going to keep it simple," continued Yagishita, apparently conscious of his friend's surroundings. "Mr Yada agreed."

Asai was unable to speak. The division chief was away from his desk, and he wasn't too afraid that the other managers and junior employees nearby might overhear, so it must have been the overwhelming relief that had taken his voice.

"Yada said that it was all fixed, but – without mentioning you, Mr Asai – I managed to invent some pretext for getting them included. Yada said that seeing as it was me, he'd make sure to get them on the tour."

"Thank you very much for that."

"Yada checked the rosters of all the agricultural co-operatives in Nagano Prefecture. It looks as if Akiharu Kido and Jiro Haruta are members of the Fujimi branch. Does that sound right?"

"Yes, that's correct. They are."

Asai felt his forehead break out in sweat. There was a throbbing in the back of his head.

"Okay, he's working on getting them on the trip. About the money – I paid him for now. It came to about 180,000 each. You can take your time paying me back. I'll stop by and get it one of these days."

"But—"

"It's complicated. Let's leave it at that for now. We'll sort it out next time we meet. Is there anything else you need to know for now?"

"Nothing in particular."

"Just to be completely clear: I can assure you that I never once mentioned your name. You can rest easy. The two men and everyone around them will think that it's Kurosaki Machinery that sent the invitation. If that's everything, then I'll let you go."

Perhaps Yagishita's cold had somehow changed his tone, but the other man's voice left a pleasant echo in Asai's ear.

That night, Asai felt more at peace than he had for a long while. The crisis had been averted; now he could depart for Nagano Prefecture on his lecture tour without any fear. If he completed this task, then he'd never be obliged to go there again. Or if he had to return, it would be at least ten years from now. Which meant never. No one would think it strange if he turned down a request that many years from now.

The 360,000 yen that Yagishita had paid Kurosaki Machinery on his behalf Asai intended to pay back in full the next time he came to Tokyo. There was a chance that the other man would tell him it was fine and not to bother returning the money, but he was normally the type to expect a return on his investments. Asai began once again to see 360,000 yen as a huge expense, but he was determined to pay it all back, no matter what Yagishita said. If you weren't meticulous with your finances, then who knew what might befall you later down the road?

Asai fell asleep, then woke up abruptly in the middle of the night. He'd got used to sleeping alone, so that wasn't the reason. Perhaps it was nerves, but even when he was asleep these days a malaise festered in his mind, which sometimes manifested itself in terrifying images. His eyes would pop open, and he wouldn't be able to get back to sleep.

If Akiharu Kido and Jiro Haruta were suddenly included in the Southeast Asia trip, wouldn't everyone back in Fujimi wonder why? Imaginations would run wild trying to guess what circumstances would have persuaded Kurosaki to add these two men to the rigorously preselected list of names. And wouldn't someone eventually suspect that it had something to do with the night of the murder, when these very men had picked up a mysterious stranger on the prefectural highway?

Damn! What if it became the topic du jour again in Fujimi, prompting yet another police investigation?

Asai had believed he'd come up with a brilliant plan, but now he realized how stupid it was. He'd been so obsessed with getting those two out of the way so he could give his Nagano lectures that he'd failed entirely to consider what the reaction of the local people might be. His stomach in knots, he sat up in his futon.

Should he call Yagishita first thing in the morning and cancel the whole thing? If he hurried, Kido and Haruta wouldn't have been told yet. There was still time to abort the plan.

But no sooner had he decided on this course of action, than he realized it would be even more dangerous. Making a request, cancelling it again... both Yagishita and Kurosaki Machinery were going to wonder what was going on. He hadn't ever explained properly why he was making the request, so a sudden cancellation now was going to look even more suspicious.

Asai couldn't sit still. His mind was in such turmoil, he thought he would go mad.

20

Worrying over nothing; making a mountain out of a mole-hill: Asai was soon to realize that this was what he'd been doing.

Akiharu Kido and Jiro Haruta were lucky enough to be chosen to participate in Kurosaki Machinery's tour of Southeast Asia. Asai received a letter from Yagishita in Kobe to tell him that they would be joining the group and leaving from Tokyo's Haneda Airport on 31 March.

> Thanks to the special care taken by the managing direc-
> tor, Mr Yada, their inclusion didn't look like a last-minute
> addition. Their friends and acquaintances back home
> have been led to believe that they were included in
> the group from the beginning. Everything went very
> smoothly and naturally.

For the time being, Asai was relieved. There was no one left wondering why Kido and Haruta had received special treatment. There was no danger they would attract the attention of gossips who might put two and two together and associate their free trip with the suspect they had given a lift to the night of the Fujimi murder case. They were no longer special cases – they were no more than two lucky members of the original group. They'd draw no extra attention, and therefore arouse nobody's suspicion.

It was a good thing that he'd stopped his scheming when he did. If he'd got the two men included on the trip only to ask for them to be removed again right away it would just have created doubts in the minds of Yagishita and Yada. They'd have examined his motives far too closely for comfort. Too many precautions would, ironically, have put him in even more danger.

He was having a nervous breakdown, Asai decided. So many unnecessary fears and concerns, one after the other. He hadn't slept at all for four or five days while he anxiously awaited the arrival of Yagishita's letter. Every time he'd been about to drift off to sleep his heart had suddenly started to palpitate and he had woken with a start. He'd try to sit up to calm himself, but the wild beating in his chest wouldn't stop and fear would stalk him under cover of darkness. Destructive thoughts would swirl round his head, and he would be seized by the urge to scream. All symptoms of neurosis.

Now that the danger had passed once more, Asai was going to have to take care of his fragile nerves. The source of his anxiety may have been removed, but the other symptoms didn't disappear so easily. They probably still lurked in the folds of his brain. There was no knowing when they might pop up and cause him to do or say something irrational. That could be serious. He would have to be extremely careful. Prudent, cautious, yet at the same time try to relax, take it easy.

Between the first and fifth of April, Asai toured around the southern part of Nagano. All of his lectures went extremely well.

The sources of his angst had now flown away, to visit Hong Kong, Macau and Taiwan. There was absolutely no chance of running into them. In his lecturer's role, he was able to talk and behave freely. He experienced a sense of liberation: his neurosis was disappearing.

After spending time at the agricultural cooperative in Chino he headed to Fujimi. The Yatsugatake mountain ridge was there in front of him. This time it was broad daylight, and he could see the line of the ridge and each fold of the range quite clearly. It was early spring, but winter still lingered up there. There was still snow on the peaks, and the slopes were tinged with brown. Under cover of night they'd seemed like a mighty barrier, dark and imposing; now the daylight exposed the desolate and rather forlorn landscape.

Whereabouts had Konosuke Kubo's corpse lain? He saw a forest in the distance, right at the opening of a valley. There must be a river over there. He'd read in the newspapers that the body had been found not far from the bank of a river, and the forest looked vaguely familiar. He could be wrong, but the shape corresponded with the image of a black mass that had stayed in his mind.

Asai looked out at the landscape from the window of the agricultural cooperative's building. It wasn't at all frightening – after all, the man was dead, his face bloodied and surrounded by three small rocks. He remembered how the stones had gleamed faintly in the dark, while the face, smashed in and covered in blood, had been virtually invisible.

"Come out, ghost of Konosuke Kubo! I dare you!" he silently shouted, his eyes fixed on a point in the distance. He wasn't afraid of ghosts. He wasn't bluffing like one of those abusive husbands who, following his poor wife's suicide, went to stare defiantly at the place she died, daring her to return as a ghost. There was nothing to fear from the dead. And in his case, he had never meant to kill Kubo. It had just happened in the heat of the moment. Kubo had exacerbated the situation with his rage and his threats, so in a way he was responsible for his own death. Was there any reason to be afraid?

Suddenly Asai realized that he'd been staring at the mountains for a while. *Stop it. The others will think you're weird,* he thought, annoyed at himself. *You have to ignore the mountains, just act normal. Don't show you feel uneasy. Take your eyes off the mountains, now.*

This odd behaviour, this kind of obsession – maybe he was having a nervous breakdown after all. *Careful, careful. Mustn't open my mouth and blurt out something bizarre. Steady now. Act normally. There's absolutely nothing to worry about. Just stay calm.*

During the whole time that he was travelling around Nagano giving his lectures, not once did he hear mention of Southeast Asia. It seemed that overseas trips were not all that unusual among agricultural cooperatives these days. Unfortunately, Japanese tour groups made up of their members had a bad reputation overseas. Still, the participants' behaviour notwithstanding, it was clear that if there were so many international tours organized for such cooperatives, then it wasn't all that special any more to be treated to a trip to Hong Kong and Taiwan.

There really was nothing to trouble himself about. No one in this area cared whether Akiharu Kido or Jiro Haruta were originally supposed to be on the tour or not. As the topic of the trip never came up, there was no discussion of its participants either.

After a very pleasant lecture tour, Asai returned on 6 April to Tokyo. His division chief thanked him for his work.

"Well done, Asai. It seems your lectures were well-received everywhere. Great job. I got a call from the Nagano prefectural union president to say how much they appreciated your work. Thank you."

With that, Asai had fulfilled his obligations. If Nagano Prefecture called again to ask him to visit, he'd be able to turn them down with a clear conscience.

The Kurosaki Machinery tour group was due to arrive back at Haneda Airport that night and return to Nagano in the morning. The schedules had worked out so that he had neatly avoided running into them.

Everything went smoothly. Yagishita confirmed it when he came up to Tokyo three days later. He and Asai went to a nearby café to talk.

"Mr Asai, I can report that the Kurosaki tour returned to Nagano on 7 April as scheduled."

"Thank you so much for arranging that."

Asai didn't want to say Kido's and Haruta's names aloud.

"The managing director, Yada, was glad to grant my request, so everything worked out fine. As I put in the letter, he managed to cover up the fact that they were added at the last minute, and I believe nobody suspected anything."

"Thank you. Thank you," Asai repeated, bowing his head.

"In the end, what he did was tell them they were replacements for someone who had to drop out."

"Replacements?"

"Yes, well, the list had been finalized. There was no other way around it, it seems. Anyway, it was done so no one would know anything about it."

That had certainly been true back in Nagano, where there had been no talk of the two men. The important thing was that they had attracted no attention. Asai decided to emphasize once again that it hadn't been his own plan.

"I'm glad I could be of use too. The person who passed the request on to me is very satisfied with the result. Actually, he asked me to pay you the money for Kido and Haruta's trip. How much is it altogether?"

"No, no. That's fine." Yagishita waved a hand in dismissal.

"I need to pay you back."

"Look, you can do that some other time."

"No, that's not right. I'll pay. I mean, not me. The money belongs to the person who asked me to sort it out."

Asai suspected that Yagishita intended to pay the full amount himself. At least that was what he seemed to be saying. Yagishita was first and foremost a businessman. He knew that the money would be an investment, bearing returns the next time he needed a favour from the ministry.

The trip had cost a total of 356,000 yen for the two participants. Asai would have been grateful if Yagishita had paid the whole sum himself. He had been quite willing, in the face of danger, to part with 500,000 or even a million yen, but now that things were calm again he felt like a fool paying such a huge sum of money for two complete strangers. He'd admonished himself once before for feeling this way, but he hadn't quite been out of the woods at that point. Now that he had nothing left to fear, it felt like a waste of money.

"Are you sure?" asked Yagishita, leaning forward a little. "If you insist, then how about paying me half the money?"

"Just half?"

"One person's travel expenses, if you like. 178,000 yen."

Yagishita was no longer offering to pay the whole thing. Asai wondered if it was the savvy negotiator in him coming out, or whether Asai himself had insisted too strongly on paying. Perhaps he should have played it more coolly, but he couldn't go back now. Anyway, he had to make out that the money wasn't his, that it had come from his mysterious client.

"Are you okay with that?" Asai produced an envelope from his jacket pocket and discreetly counted the 10,000-yen bills inside.

"Sure. If it was your money then I wouldn't accept it, but as it came from someone else, I'll just take half." The broad grin on Yagishita's face seemed to suggest that he'd be fine with Asai using the other half of the sum as pocket money.

Asai handed him seventeen of the 10,000-yen notes, and then, having no smaller notes to make up the exact amount, he added one more 10,000 note. But Yagishita tried to return it.

"Sorry, I don't have any change either. Don't worry, 170,000 is enough."

"No, I couldn't... I mean —"

"Come on, Mr Asai. What's a little 10,000-yen bill between friends?"

Akiharu Kido and Jiro Haruta were extremely grateful to have been chosen to participate in a tour of Southeast Asia sponsored by Kurosaki Machinery, even if they did only make the cut as replacements. Kido wasn't exactly one of the more powerful officials at the Fujimi agricultural co-operative. He was just an ordinary member of the council. Haruta was no more than a junior clerk in the coopera-tive's sales department. They were delighted to have the opportunity to travel abroad in the company of so many influential people from various districts throughout Japan. At the same time, they were puzzled at the imbalance in status between the others and themselves.

That said, the men made no connection between the invitation and any criminal intent. On the contrary: they wanted to find out who had been thoughtful enough to offer them this preferential treatment so they could thank him properly. They were honest, dutiful types.

As soon as they returned to Nagano, the two men wrote a letter to the managing director of Kurosaki Machinery, the most senior of the people who came to see the group off at Haneda Airport. The letter was handed to him in person by one of his staff members.

In his reply, Mr Yada made it clear that it was Mr Yagishita, the president of Yagishita Ham in Kobe, who had been responsible for getting the two men on the tour, and that Yagishita had paid their costs personally. He felt obliged to admit that it hadn't been his own company that had paid for the two men, and to let them know of the other man's generosity.

Naturally, Kido and Haruta did the right thing. They set off immediately for Kobe, to thank Yagishita personally for his kindness and take him a souvenir they had purchased in Hong Kong. All the while, they couldn't grasp why someone with whom they had absolutely no connection had taken it upon himself to pay for their overseas travel.

Yagishita, for his part, was embarrassed when the two men entered his office and bowed so low to him. He'd only paid half of their travel expenses; in other words, only one of the two men was in debt to his kindness. Asai had paid for the other one, and it pained Yagishita to have both men thank him so wholeheartedly.

And with that, Yagishita broke his promise to Asai. He explained that their real benefactor was Assistant Division Chief Tsuneo Asai at the Ministry of Agriculture and Forestry. You couldn't really blame Yagishita. It was too uncomfortable for him to accept the effusive thanks from the two men all by himself.

"But you really don't need to thank Mr Asai. He was asked to do the favour by someone else, who insists on remaining anonymous. I'll contact Mr Asai myself to let him know how grateful you are."

But Kido and Haruta really were conscientious types. Even more so when they heard that their secret benefactor was an assistant division chief at the Ministry of Agriculture. On their way back from Kobe, they didn't change trains at Nagoya to head up to Nagano. They stayed on board and travelled straight to Tokyo.

Arriving in Kasumigaseki around three in the afternoon, they went up to the reception desk at the Ministry of Agriculture and Forestry. Presenting their business cards, they requested a meeting with Assistant Division Chief Tsuneo Asai. After being asked to wait a while, the reply came that Mr Asai was very busy and wouldn't be able to meet with them.

However, their sense of obligation was very strong. They thought it would be impolite just to leave a letter of thanks, and decided to wait in the reception area until Asai left the ministry at the end of the day. Country folks are incredibly patient. Asai had absolutely no idea that they would wait for him, and assumed the two men would have left long ago. So much so that he didn't even bother to slip out of the back door but instead came walking out through the main foyer with all the other employees at the normal finishing time of 5.40 p.m.

The receptionist, feeling sorry for the two men who had waited so long, pointed Asai out to them. They tried to approach him, but there was such a crowd of people leaving the ministry that they couldn't get to him right away. In the confusion, Asai ended up outside. The two men rushed after him, and Akiharu Kido called out.

"Mr Asai! Mr Asai!"

Asai stopped abruptly and turned around.

Kido approached Asai, who seemed frozen to the spot, his features petrified. Haruta came up and joined him. The two men bowed in unison.

"Are you Assistant Division Chief Tsuneo Asai? I'm Akiharu Kido from the Fujimi agricultural cooperative.

This is my colleague, Jiro Haruta. We enquired after you at the reception desk but heard you were very busy. However, we really wanted to meet you, so we decided to wait —"

In the middle of Kido's greeting a very odd thing happened. Asai suddenly let out a bizarre scream, as if he'd been physically assaulted, and set off running. He ran fast, his body leaning forward at such a sharp angle that he almost dropped his briefcase.

Dumbfounded, the two men watched him take off. What was going on? What had they done? They hadn't a clue, but out of the vague idea that there must have been some kind of misunderstanding between Asai and themselves, they took off after him, Kido yelling as he ran.

"Mr Asai! Mr Asai! Wait! Just a minute!"

But instead of stopping, Asai ran even faster. At this time of the evening, there were crowds of people coming out of the other ministries in Kasumigaseki, and heads were turning to look. It was mid-April, around six o'clock in the evening; the light had faded and night was setting in. As he continued to flee, the headlights of passing cars lit Asai from the rear.

Giving up the chase, the two men stopped and watched him make his deranged getaway. But that figure in the headlights – they had a similar memory from not so long ago... The hurrying figure, backlit by their headlights, on the prefectural highway near Yatsugatake. That night on their way home from a meeting... Didn't Mr Asai have the exact same curve to his back?

"No! It couldn't have been the assistant division chief, could it?"

Kido and Haruta talked about the incident all the way home on the train, and even more once they were back in Nagano. They weren't sure what to believe.

The rumour quickly reached the Fujimi police, who made their move. Investigators came to Tokyo to question Tsuneo Asai as to where he had been on the night of Konosuke Kubo's murder.

There may not have been prints left on the hair oil bottle – in fact, there was a complete absence of material or physical evidence – but the police knew that investigating a suspect's alibi was the way to break a case. They knew from experience that it never failed.